T0197303

# The WAY of the DOG

## From The Memoirs of Eros, the Metaphysical Dog

Eva A. MacDonnell

iUniverse

# THE WAY OF THE DOG
# FROM THE MEMOIRS OF EROS, THE METAPHYSICAL DOG

*This is a work of fiction. All of the characters, names, incidents, organizations, and dialogue in this novel are either the products of the author's imagination or are used fictitiously.*

*iUniverse books may be ordered through booksellers or by contacting:*

*iUniverse*
*1663 Liberty Drive*
*Bloomington, IN 47403*
*www.iuniverse.com*
*1-800-Authors (1-800-288-4677)*

*Because of the dynamic nature of the Internet, any web addresses or links contained in this book may have changed since publication and may no longer be valid. The views expressed in this work are solely those of the author and do not necessarily reflect the views of the publisher, and the publisher hereby disclaims any responsibility for them.*

*Any people depicted in stock imagery provided by Getty Images are models, and such images are being used for illustrative purposes only. Certain stock imagery © Getty Images.*

*ISBN: 978-1-5320-5912-4 (sc)*
*ISBN: 978-1-5320-5913-1 (hc)*
*ISBN: 978-1-5320-5911-7 (e)*

*Library of Congress Control Number: 2018912476*

*Print information available on the last page.*

*iUniverse rev. date: 11/02/2018*

To Krysta and Shiri, my life coaches. Or am I theirs?

# CONTENTS

# DOGDOM DISCLAIMER

You may not believe this, but this is a work of fiction. Really! The names of dogs, characters (human partners), inferior beasts (farm animals, insects, etc.), businesses, places, events, and incidents are either the product of the author's imagination or used in a purely doggy fictitious Way.

No dogs, humans, or farm animals have been harmed in any way during the production of this book. (I'm not sure about wild animals. They reside beyond my ken.) Resemblance to imagined or actual creatures or events is purely coincidental, except when they are not. In other words, any resemblance to actual dogs, persons, or gods, living or dead—except, of course, Eros—is an unanswerable philosophical question.

Being in this book, Eros will live on long beyond when we are all gone. So Eros the dog will become Eros the metaphysical dog, mythic and immortal, which arguably makes him more existential than all of us.

# IN THE BEGINNING

I n the beginning, all was dark and silent.
*I am a pup,* Eros thought as he opened his eyes on the fifth day of his life for the first time and beheld the golden sheen of a furry mountain. Over this horizon rose a face of immense proportions with drooping ears on either side. Eros's curiosity, soon to be his trademark, inspired an inquiry. *How do I know this?*

"Hello, Eros," a gentle voice rang in Eros's mind. He cocked his head to the side, not quite knowing what was happening, but of course, all this was new and far beyond his experiences since he had none. With a flopping tongue framed by a great smile, the apparition continued, "I'm your mother! Welcome to the universe!"

With this pronouncement, a flood of thoughts entered Eros's mind, providing him with an understanding of what a mother was.

Eros stammered mentally, *But you're so big!*

"It's all relative, my dear," his mother stated. "When you are small, I will seem very large. But when you are a grown-up, fearsome hound, you will be bigger than me, and I will appear small."

"What?" Eros exclaimed, jostled by other small, squiggling bodies. He became aware that he was with four other small creatures that were like him, cradled within his mother's curled body.

"Those are your brothers and sisters, Eros," his mother obliged, answering his question even before he fully formed it.

"Where do all my thoughts about mothers come from?" Eros picked through the mental images and feelings that flooded his mind, describing what a mother was.

"That's how we communicate. Dogs speak by thinking to one another telepathically. Right now, there is nothing to be afraid of. You can't learn if you don't listen, so just listen!" his mother assured him. "The simple answer is that this is how we talk, unlike humans."

"Talk?" Eros tried to focus, but confusion blurred his thoughts.

"We are dogs, Eros," his mother began. "Miniature golden poodles! The most wonderful thing about dogs is that we communicate telepathically, a fact unknown to humans."

"Oh." Eros pretended that he knew what his mother was talking about. His infant mind was not very orderly, so he bounced to another subject. "What's a human?"

"Humans are creatures doomed to walk on their hind legs. They look so uncomfortable doing so!" his mother explained. Again, a blast of thoughts entered his mind, projecting the image of a woman named Mary. "And they are handicapped when it comes to telepathy."

"They must struggle mightily to communicate," Eros figured.

"Yes, they do! You will see a real human soon, my partner, Mary. They are ugly creatures that come in many colors and shapes. They are as ungainly as they are ugly because they walk on two paws while using the other two paws to move things around." Mother continued to stuff knowledge into Eros. She was amazed at how much her pup absorbed at such an early age. "But humans can also be our best friends if they are properly trained."

"Trained?" Eros's head was spinning. There was so much for him to learn.

"Humans are clever creatures, but most of the time, they think they know more than they do. Humans need to be taught how to know less. Regrettably, it takes time, patience, and a good dog for them to achieve wisdom."

"You said humans aren't telepathic?" Eros's questions flowed like a river. His mother was impressed. This question reached back into an earlier part of their conversation, which for most pups would be long forgotten by this time in one so young.

"Humans have some telepathy but mainly talk to one another by making sounds, grunts, groans, clicks, and snorts. It's very unbecoming. Their telepathy is very primitive." Eros's mother waited for a few seconds, adding a dramatic pause to emphasize her next sentence. "Being highly advanced creatures, dogs, on the other hand, use the graceful method of talking without making sounds, by speaking directly from mind to mind."

"Do we make sounds at all when we talk?"

"Every now and then, if our emotions are stimulated, we bark or growl." His mother smiled. "I've heard you munchkins occasionally growling when you are feeding, but being so young, you probably didn't notice."

"Why are humans that way and we this way?" Eros was relentless.

"It's the Way of the dog, how we developed, where we come from, and what we think," Mother replied patiently. "Humans just developed differently."

"Where did I come from?" Eros asked, turning the question from dogs to himself.

"You were born!" his mother replied, and somehow, he knew the entire process, starting with the initial impregnation. Dogs are not burdened with a sense of shame or impropriety. The images floating through his mind from his mother were graphic, but overall, Eros came away with a clear idea of his physical origins.

"Are you done?" Eros replied. "Did I need to learn all that now?"

"You are insisting on learning everything at once," his mother said softly. "This is how our telepathy and our mingling works."

"Mingling?" Eros was like a machine rattling off question after question.

"I was hoping to explain this to you when you were a bit older." His mother reluctantly continued her explanation, resigning herself to this persistent questioning by her new puppy. "Our minds mingled. I touched your mind with my thoughts. Mingling is imperfect, but this method is how dogs transfer knowledge from generation to generation. Unfortunately, more often than not, you get more than you want."

"What is mind?"

"My, my! Aren't you the metaphysical one?"

"What is metaphysical?"

"Metaphysics is the search for ultimate reality."

"What is ultimate reality?"

"If I knew what ultimate reality was," Mother said, lolling out her tongue, "then no one would have to search for it."

This was a lot for a little pup to take in.

"Why am I metaphysical?"

"Because metaphysicists always ask a lot of questions but never find what they are looking for."

"Huh?" Now this little pup was definitely perplexed.

"You could ask me a hundred questions right now." His mother wagged her tail. "And I could give you a hundred answers, but you would still have a hundred questions more for me. Although there is no end to your questions, you will find answers are not so accommodating."

This information overload was overpowering Eros's faculties during his first brush with consciousness. Much of his mother's words were floating by like some uncapturable wisp on the wind. Questions upon questions were building up in his little brain until he was ready to burst, but his eyes began to droop against his wishes.

"So metaphysicians ask endless questions, never expecting to get all the answers?" Eros got this question out, but being five days old, he was fighting off sleep since he did not have a lot of stamina.

This rush of new thoughts, impressions, and images was starting to overwhelm the little pup. Sleep encroached on his awareness. It seemed his whole world was spinning with new objects and ideas. Of course, everything was new, but this urgency to sleep was dampening his desires and the speed of his thoughts.

"Yes, sort of!" His mother observed the obvious. "It's like Hydra, a nine-headed serpent. If you cut off one head, two grow back. Metaphysicians ask one question and get an answer, metaphorically cutting off one of the heads of the serpent of ignorance only to have two questions emerge, two new heads, to take the place of the first question."

"Questions and answers?" Eros asked.

"Yes, but I do give metaphysicians some credit," his mother admitted. "For all their questions, their ultimate goal is to understand happiness."

"What is this?" Eros queried. "I can't keep my eyes open."

"Eros, that is normal. Even though we've been chatting less than five minutes, you are getting tired. You are about to nap." His mother nodded her huge head with her floppy ears and a wide smile.

"Will I wake up?" Eros was distressed. He recalled that he had woken from what felt to him like an almost endless sleep, the sleep before birth.

"This sleep will pass, and when you wake, you will be ready to romp. The Big Nap is the sleep you come from when you are born and go to when you die. This time, and for a long time, you are going to take short naps. Hopefully, you won't go for the Big Nap for a very long time."

"Will I remember any of this?" Eros realized he didn't recall any memories before this morning.

"Actually, you've woken up several times already, but your eyes were closed. It must have seemed like a dark dream to you." His mother acknowledged silently that Eros was a smart little dog. Not knowingly, she allowed this thought of pride to pass between their two telepathic minds, her admiration seeping through the mingling. "Apparently, your story is about to begin, a life of asking questions and hopefully, seeking joy and happiness. As for now, although you may remember some or all or none of our talk, you will remember my love."

With a jar, Eros felt a profusion of golden bubbles titillating his consciousness, the love of his mother glowing gently all around him. Cuddled in the curl of his mother's golden furry body, he felt a radiance entering his thoughts, making his whole world luminous with a soft golden light. Having no distractions to burden him, Eros was able to perceive that this light of love was just a veil, beyond which this great source for Everything was nearby, emanating pure joy.

Eros felt his mother's happiness define his existence. His mother was right. Eros never forgot this moment, even when he was an old dog on the doorstep of death. Joy was the greatest thing that he was introduced to on his first day of consciousness, and it would be the final thing that he would remember on his last day.

# EROS'S FIRST HUMAN

Three days of eating, sleeping, and not a lot of thinking went by. Unlike that first day with his mother, life was not intellectually stimulating, just a blur of feeding and snoozing. Eros had no sense of time, so he had no idea how much time had gone by. The disorder of randomly napping, waking, and bumping heads with his siblings was messy and not to his liking.

Eros did open his eyes and his mind, to his great relief, that his mother's assessment of the Big Nap was accurate. Again and again, he woke on the following days with a satisfactory modicum of sentience and regularity. Consistency bred confidence. Eros figured that if something was consistent, then it was real, and this concept became a cornerstone of his reality, even though he did not know it.

During this extended time of awakening, Eros got familiar with his companions. There was Wanda, Artemis, Charley, and Matt, two females and two males. Eros knew this because males and females had different smells and from this recognition he discovered that he was a male.

Sometimes these squabbles were fun, just pushing and shoving, but at times they became more intense in keeping with how hungry the pups were. The more frantic battles occurred after their mother was away, and the five of them were left clumped together to keep warm. When the pups were together like that, hunger eventually set in, and they all began whimpering and looking, some with unseeing, unopened eyes. When their mother did return, their ravenous and desperate scramble was anything but pretty.

Since Eros's eyes had not fully developed, all he could see was that they were in a fuzzy valley. One time when their mother was away, being a bit more curious than his brothers and sisters, he wandered from their cuddling mass into this fuzzy world. This exploration ended when he bumped into a wall. This edifice was huge by Eros's calculation, using his small body as the yardstick. The brown walls went off upward beyond where he could see, past his hazy horizon, and Everything was so big to him.

As Eros looked up, a monstrous squiggling mass, fingers writhing, slipped through the fuzzy reality, breaching the edges of his perception. He thought the object looked like an octopus, and he wondered how he even knew about an octopus. Whatever it was, these thrashing tentacles made Eros most apprehensive.

"Where are you going, little guy?" These words came booming through the fuzz, and then the grappling monster thing grabbed him, raising him high. His perspective on this fuzzy world changed. Eros's brothers and sisters were no longer part of his universe, and this huge, wide face without any fur and a missing muzzle, framed by a bunch of squiggly white and gray hair appeared before him. Since then, he discovered that he had been clasped in a hand. This was Eros's first human contact, as foretold by his mother, with a lithe, older woman named Mary. The woman shouted, "Aren't you the curious one?"

These words boomed out of the woman's mouth. Eros was not used to such a raucous method of communication, even though he had been forewarned by his mother.

"Can you not yell at me?" Eros asked, but the woman acted as if she could not hear his telepathic message.

"You're so cute!"

Again with the booming! Eros could hear the words from the great, hulking woman's voice, while simultaneously, the words blasted in his brain. Even though the woman could not read Eros's thought, he could telepathically read hers. It was obvious that she could not read his thoughts.

*Why is she making sounds to imitate words that he can hear in his brain? Are these the grunts and groans humans use to communicate that his mother had told him about?* Eros questioned, declaring, "It's so inefficient!"

"She can't hear your thoughts, Eros. At least not very well," he heard his mother say, even though he could not see her. "Those sounds are her speaking what is in her thoughts as if she was reading a cue card. Humans are unable to commune telepathically as we do."

"Yes, you mentioned this before," Eros acknowledged. Having been picked up and handled for the first time, he was understandably nervous but also perplexed. He asked anxiously, "Should I be afraid?"

"No, Eros, don't be afraid!" His mother assured him. "Mary is my partner. She thinks she owns me, but no one can own someone else, especially a dog. Anyone who thinks that way is deluded. Nevertheless, I let her think that because it is a comfort to her. From what I can tell, humans like to be deluded. Let Mary pet you and kiss you. You will even like it…eventually."

And the woman did pet Eros, stroking his back gently. He had a bunch of knots in his muscles because he tensed at the woman's initial touch. However, the woman calmed him down, and the tension seeped out of his body. This was his first massage by a human, and he did like it.

"I could get used to this," Eros thought.

"I did," Mother interjected. "If you get a good human, you can train them to give you massages whenever you want!"

Then the woman contorted her face into a terrible state, her lips bunching up as if she was going to suck him up and consume him in one messy slurp.

"What is *that*!" Eros screamed mentally, cringing at this gross apparition.

"Don't worry," Mother comforted him. "Mary is puckering up to kiss you."

"What's a—Egad!" Eros exclaimed. Even after his mother's assurances, he was freaking out as Mary brought him to her crumpled lips. There was a smacking, wet, puffing sound, and she was done. Relieved, Eros found that he was not hurt, although his dignity was a bit disheveled. Afterward, Mary petted him again.

"That was a kiss!" Mother answered his abbreviated question. "Humans are not advanced like us. They don't know how to show affection without being messy like this."

"They don't know how to nuzzle or touch noses?" Eros was astounded.

"No, although occasionally, they cuddle," Mother confirmed, proffering a theory. "I don't think humans' noses are as sensitive as ours. Poor things, they can't know true pleasure!"

"That's sad." For the first time, Eros felt the feeling of sadness.

"It is rumored that some people do rub noses, but this is rare, I understand." Mother spoke authoritatively. "Mary watches a lot of nature shows, and I remember seeing Eskimos rubbing noses. I didn't realize that a human society could be so advanced."

"What's she doing now?" Eros squirmed, feeling his stomach drop as the woman's hands were moving downward rapidly.

"Don't worry. She is just putting you back down in the box," Mother informed him. "Enjoy the ride!"

With that, Mary's fingers closed lightly about him, and with her hands tilted, she lowered Eros precipitously. He was filled with an odd mixture of fear and exhilaration. Although he had never been on one, it felt like being on a roller coaster.

"I've been on one," his mother answered his unspoken question. "Roller coasters can be fun!"

"Odd that I know about it," Eros thought. He had not felt any overt mingling.

"Mingling between dogs can easily seep through at any time on anything the mingler has thought or seen, especially in the last forty-eight hours, unless an effort is made to hide your thoughts. It's called mingle mangling, when other thoughts than what you want to say go over at the same time," his mother informed him, turning pensive.

"Yes, like when I knew about octopuses and didn't know how I knew it?"

"Yes, but as you grow older you can control your mingling, and prevent anyone from seeing your thoughts, unless you're under great stress." Skylark surveyed her inquisitive little puppy. "My, my, you know more now about mingling than all the rest of the pups will know in weeks."

This conversation was all happening while Eros was careening downward. His fuzzy boundaries clarified, and he could see a box come into view with his four siblings inside. The cardboard box sat on an off-white linoleum floor. Dropped within the middle of his puppy pack, Eros cuddled within the comfort of his own mother's body. Around him, he could hear the puppies whining for food.

"Come on, Shyla. Time for you to get to work," Mary boomed.

"Mother?"

"Yes, Mary calls me Shyla, but my name is really Skylark," Mother answered Eros's unfinished question. "She almost has my name right. Mary's poor telepathic ability is remarkably good for a human, and she heard my name as Shyla when we imprinted."

"What's imprinting?"

"That is when you meet your human minion—er, partner." Mother reworded her statement. Something about being politically correct was all Eros understood concerning this semantic reconfiguration. "Humans need training! Good ones are soft and wet like water pouring into a bowl."

"Why do we need humans?"

"We don't. We can survive as nicely in the Wild as with a human, but we took pity on poor humanity. They are such lost creatures." Mother sniffed. "They needed our help, so dogdom decided to take on the burden of leading these poor creatures out of the wilderness with the hope that they would listen to our wisdom, at least every now and then. The beginning of this process is the imprint, but the end results have been mixed."

"Do you let a human brand you?" Eros mind went racing ahead. Somewhere in his thoughts had erupted an image of a large beast called a cow being burned with an identifying mark.

"No," Skylark said and laughed. "Stop reading my thoughts too deeply. We brand them, the humans, but telepathically, not with hot irons. When we get together with our designated human, you need to telepathically stare at them until their thoughts acquiesce to your bidding. You want food, and the human gets it for you. You want to be let out, and the human opens the door for you."

"All because you imprint your mind on theirs?"

"Yes, it is like synchronizing their thoughts to yours." Mother nodded. "I particularly like taking Mary for a walk in the city."

"City?"

"I know you have not seen a city before." Eros received a new mingling of images. "The city is a universe of boxes in boxes like Mary's house, but they reach all the way to heaven. There are a lot of humans, and they do a lot of talking. But they just babble, and it is rare when they ever really understand one another. Well, I like taking Mary for a walk to show her off to all the other dogs in the neighborhood."

"That sounds nice," Eros commented. "Sounds like you are proud of Mary."

"She has responded to my training well." Mother sounded very pleased with herself. "One of the keys of the training is that the human must think they are in charge. Consequently, I let Mary attach a leash to me and allow her the illusion that she is in control. The leash is actually to make sure the human doesn't wander away. Humans are so easy to train, if you remember that they have short attention spans."

"Okay, so no collar for humans—only leashes." Eros attempted to nail down this factoid. "And I make sure my human is oblivious to my control."

"Eros, it's not that hard. Humans are easy to subjugate," Mother assured him. "People are just big puppies looking to be told where to go."

"Weren't we talking about imprinting?" Eros was gnawing on this topic as if he had a bone.

"Yes, I diverge," his mother admitted. "You can tell how well the imprinting went by how close your human gets your name. Your name emerges from who you are, which is why my name is Skylark, because I love running and leaping into the sky like a bird. When I was a puppy, I felt like I could fly!"

"If the imprinting goes bad," Mother gloomily surmised. "Your human would call you Fido or Butch or Dog, and you can't help your human to find happiness. This is immensely sad, and these humans get angry and can do unmentionable things like abandon or beat you."

"That's not good," Eros bemoaned the downside of this picture. He didn't realize that he had made an initial foray into the foothills of good and bad as he roamed in the shadows of the mountains of right and wrong.

"Dogs can't control everything, and humans less," Mother confirmed. "But dogs are always optimistic, and our prime directive is to survive because if you survive, you can find your way back to happiness."

"What's happiness?"

"You are the curious one," Eros's mother said as she leaped into the box and into his field of vision. When Eros finally saw his mother appear in the box, hunger took over his thoughts as Mary gently put him down in the midst of the pups. Settling in among these squirming bodies, Eros had no other thoughts to share, and his fleeting questions had flown. The last thing he remembered before feeding were words from his mother.

"Eros, you have a lot to learn."

# THE UNIVERSE

These early days passed quickly. Eros slept a lot, ate a lot, and slept some more. His very early window of lucidity blurred into a movie that was running a bit too fast to be seen clearly. After that initial day of sentience, days passed into a nuzzling and napping limbo. Eros awoke on his ninth day to another period of clarity and curiosity, which led to another exchange with his mother.

"Mama?" Eros peeped, entangled in a pile of puppies.

"Yes, Eros?"

"You mentioned the universe," Eros tentatively inquired. Somehow from his first encounter with sentience, he had learned some vague thoughts about what reality was, but sometimes the idea of Everythingness was like a teat lost in his mother's fur. "What is the universe?"

"That is a *big* question for a little pup," his mother murmured, not wanting to wake the other sleeping pups. Dogs with pups are just like humans in this regard. *Don't wake sleeping babies!*

"I see the sky, and it is white," Eros insisted. From his perspective, his sky was the white ceiling of the room. "Is that the edge of the universe?"

"It takes courage to ask questions," his mother said and smiled in her thoughts. She presented this rhetorical statement so she could have time to think of an answer to his question. "This must mean you are my most courageous pup!"

"Are the sides of the universe always brown?" His mother's comment pleased Eros, but he was a dog on a mission and would not be swayed.

"Eros, the universe is boxes within boxes like the city I told you about. You are in a small box," Mother capitulated to Eros's insistence, and answered as best as she could. "A cardboard box!"

"The sky?"

"The sky you think you see right now is the ceiling, which is painted white." Mother explained. "That's the top of this box and the top of the next box as well."

"Oh, the ceiling." Eros's response oozed with awe.

"But this is a wee little box, Eros," his mother continued. "Soon you will be turned out into the next universe, which is a larger box with many boxes inside that are called rooms. This universe is called a house."

Eros was speechless!

"This is the universe, where order reigns!" his mother confidently declared. "Our little box is a microcosm of the universe where dogs are warm and safe and fed and live without any concerns. A paradise satisfying all our needs."

"So the universe represents a cosmic order?"

"Yes, but there is the *Wild!*" Mother declared ominously.

"Oh," Eros responded apprehensively to his mother's tone of thought. "Don't you mean the wild?"

""I don't capitalize my words without reason. For example, Everythingness is capitalized because it includes the seen and unseen." Skylark admonished. "Likewise, the Wild includes the unseen beyond the wild, and it is Wild!"

"Oh," Eros thought this a wondrous explanation.

"Philosophers named it ultimate reality. In fact, the door in the kitchen leads to the Wild; it's also called the Great Box." His mother spoke this in hushed tones as if it were a horror story. "The Great Box has a blue ceiling with white specs that at times get so populous that the ceiling turns white just like in here or dark gray, even black on a stormy day."

His mother paused for effect, and Eros, being just a pup, was affected.

"The Wild cannot be controlled. Anyone who thinks otherwise is a fool!" Mother resumed. "And anything that can't be controlled is outside our universe. Let me try drawing this for you."

To Eros great surprise, an image popped into his head, a visual projected by his mother. He recalled this had happened before on the day of his first awakening, but he had forgotten about this process. The image was a large circle with a small circle inside. The inside circle was labeled "the universe," while the rest of the interior of the large circle was identified as "the Wild."

"The circle encircling the universe is like wallpaper. A thin layer separates the universe from the Wild, which you can see in reality as the dirt under your paws or the blue sky above. The illusion is that there is perfect order within our universe. Beyond this perfection, a thin transition layer exists, outside of which all of the potential things that can happen churns in chaotic confusion. Behind this curtain, the Wild lingers with death, destruction, and the mindless timelessness of Nothingness."

"Will that wall cover ever collapse?"

"Openings occur. When these weaknesses happen, terrible creatures sneak in and danger lurks!" His mother confirmed. "You want to be as close to the center of the universe when that happens, and the universe can protect you!"

"Why is the universe order?"

"The universe is what we know," his mother stated, but she was starting to feel uneasy. She'd had one previous owner and now Mary, and neither of them could be called intellectual giants. (In fact, her first owner was an intellectual moron.)

As can be surmised, her concept of the universe was homegrown and primitive, but sometimes the simple can make more sense than the complex and sophisticated. Eros's questions were starting to make his mother nervous since they were making her simple description more complex, exploring areas she had never explored. As Eros expanded his mother's vision of the universe, the less sense it seemed to make.

"So the universe is our knowledge?" Eros fought with his mother's concepts. "The universe is our mind?"

"*No!*" His mother realized her explanation had fallen short. Exasperated, she responded with more force than she intended, exposing her growing insecurity. "The universe is real, not a figment of any imagination!"

His mother may not have noticed that her picture of the universe was cracking under the pressure of Eros's questions, but her feelings did. With this attack on her philosophical roots, his mother became more emotional. She had invested a lifetime of thought into her theory of the universe, and this theory, which framed a grand portrait of her reality, was under attack. By a pup no less!

"What is mind?" Eros could have sworn he had asked this before, but his memory was still developing.

"Hercules would call you Cerberus with a question barking from each of your three heads!" His mother was visibly upset. "Eros, I forbid you to ask any more questions about the universe today!"

"Hercules?"

"No more questions today. *I forbid it!*" Every creature comes up with their own unified theory of the universe, one that gives them great comfort. Unfortunately, if you take the theory away, the comfort goes away too. "I need a break."

With this final declaration, his mother got up, shook off the pups still hanging on her, and jumped out of their box, visibly upset.

*Aren't mothers supposed to be smarter than their children? At least for a little while?* Skylark thought.

# THE FUZZY WORLD AND ME

The next few days were just a lot of feeding and sleeping. Eros's explorations outside the box were curtailed, other than Mary plucking him and his siblings up to pet and kiss them. Eros continued to dislike the messy kissing, and he wasn't alone in his feelings.

"Argh! Not again!" Eros groaned when Mary picked him up. The other pups giggled in the background, relieved that the complaint was not from them.

"You're so cute!" Mary liked to pick the puppies up, and she used their cuteness as her excuse. Eros took great umbrage at this label for him, being a fierce, proud little dog. Magnanimously, Eros let Mary get away with this affront, but he was not a happy pup when she brought the excuse up. Eros also caught her rationalizing that she had to pick all the pups up to help *domesticate* them.

"Such nonsense!" Eros would blurt out when Mary thought this, but only his mother and siblings could hear him. Except for this flaw, Mary was a nice lady, but the other dogs could hear Eros grumbling. "Humans need to be domesticated, not dogs!"

Even though his bark was small and his bite nonexistent, Eros was a vicious little doggie. He felt it demeaning to be mollycoddled. Eros could see no way that this woman could sway his primal tendencies, yet slowly, he learned to trust Mary. Regardless, he would never admit his bark was less loud or his bite less lethal. Eros still contended that he was never domesticated, but he did become more civilized.

Soon Eros even looked forward to the petting, but never those loud kisses. The massages compensated for this woman's messy smooches. With five puppies, doing the massages and the kisses more than once a day for each pup did not happen often. Before life dispersed the pups to various futures, against his instinctual nature, Eros learned to like Mary a lot.

"I am forever a wild puppy at heart," Eros declared to himself.

A couple of days later, Eros's eyesight developed enough to clear up the fuzziness at the current limits of his vision. He could see the sides of the box right up to the top of the partitions, and he felt he knew everything that anyone could ever need to know about the universe. Eros's universe was a box into which his mother jumped in and out of, and Mary's hands dipped into on occasion.

Eros's mother was so wise and brave that she could transcend the limits of all knowledge and leap without fear into the unknown, far beyond the universe that he knew. He was so proud of her, braving the Wild and then jumping back into his crystal clear world.

Since his mother had a few days to compose herself, Eros marshaled up his courage to bring up the universe once again.

"Mother, the universe is a box," Eros stated. "Aren't you afraid of jumping out of the box of the universe?"

"No, no, Eros!" Not showing any sign of angst, Skylark was more prepared for Eros's barrage of questions as she chuckled, amused at Eros's naiveté. "This *is* just a box, but beyond this box, the universe is made of more boxes, as I told you before."

"Wow," Eros said, awestruck. He felt stupid, realizing he had forgotten this. Obviously, his memory abilities were still in development.

"Yes," his mother said, nodding her all-knowing head, acknowledging Eros's lapse in memory. "Mary calls the next box a house. The house is actually a box with many boxes in it, which Mary calls rooms. Oddly, once you leave the house, the next box hangs off the side of this house and is called the kennel, which ironically is smaller than this house."

*Going bigger to smaller seems inconsistent.* Thinking this over silently, Eros did not express his views. His mother was so wise. He concluded that he must be wrong. Plus he recalled the last time he challenged his mother's views; the response was not welcoming.

Not everyone knows the limits of their universe, and his mother was so certain that she knew hers. She had no doubts, so she had to be right. (Later, Eros would understand that anyone with no doubts should find some.)

"And you remember the city of boxes? They are houses built on top of houses, boxes on top of boxes."

"So complex!" Eros blurted out, dumbstruck.

"And they are *big* rooms," Skylark declared. "Bigger than you can imagine!"

This conversation became stilted as Eros was flabbergasted and unable to speak. His mother waited patiently during this pause, glad Eros was not asking more difficult questions...or any questions for that matter.

"You've mentioned the Wild a number of times." Eros almost stuttered. "And I don't know what the Wild is. Is it just chaos?"

"Yes, the Wild is the thing beyond everything, the box of all boxes, beyond the control of anything," Skylark spoke in hushed tones, as if the Wild could listen in on them. "Beyond the universe is eternal chaos, and that is called the W*ild*!"

Mother emphasized the last word as if it should be the last word. Being metaphysically inclined, for Eros, there was never a last word on any subject.

"The Wild is uncontrollable Everythingness?" Eros timidly asked.

"Yes, and out of the nothingness, monsters come to eat little puppies!" This was Skylark's new strategy. If you can't beat them, scare them! This tactic worked for a while. Eros paused, contemplating all that his mother had said.

"When I woke from the Big Nap," Eros said, breaking his silence, referring to the time before he was born, "I found the universe to be fuzzy, but now I can see very clearly the walls and ceiling of this room. Some are parts of the cardboard box, and some are not."

"You are maturing." Mother was glad to move on to a new subject. "In the next few weeks, your senses of seeing, hearing, touching through your whiskers, and especially smelling, will develop. You will see a small spider on the ceiling as if it were right in front of you!"

"That's wonderful," Eros exclaimed. "So the fuzzy universe will no longer be fuzzy?"

"As long as you stay out of the Wild, everything you sense will be as clear as if seen through a polished crystal glass."

"And I'll remember it?" Eros was irritated when he forgot things.

"Like your senses, your memory will increase functionally, and for some, exceptionally so."

"Will I be able to stay out of the Wild?" Eros wondered.

"Probably not," Skylark had to admit.

# TIPPING THE UNIVERSE

E ros's first two weeks were eventful in a quiet way. The light around the box returned regularly, and Eros marveled at this. His mother referred to this repetition of first light as "morning" and associated it with the start of a new day. While Eros was pondering the magnificence of this regularity of natural reality, he was unaware that his life was about to change when Mary appeared.

"Hello, kiddos!" Mary strode into view and leaned over, framing her huge face in the opening at the top of the box. "Time for you to open your horizons!"

With that statement, Eros's whole universe shook and was uplifted. He felt like his reality was turning upside down. Mary had picked the whole box up and started walking with it. The puppies' universe was swaying as Mary strolled with the box in her arms.

"Now that you guys and gals are moving around a bit, it's time to move you to the kennel." Mary announced her intentions, stating patronizingly, "As if you have a clue, since you don't know what I am talking about!"

Eros was offended. This was the first time Eros encountered human arrogance. Mary exposed the false sentiment that her human knowledge was greater than a dog's. Even during the time when his whole universe was turning and twisting in Mary's hands, he was stunned by this condescension.

"Shyla, come," Mary boomed her thoughts and words over the puppies. (Fortunately, Eros had learned to better control the multiple perceptions of Mary's vocal sounds and telepathic shouts. Pretty soon he would not notice them at all.)

"*Mother!*" Wanda, Charley, Artemis, and Matt exclaimed as one, alarmed by the turn of events.

"Yes, children," Mother exclaimed. "Don't be alarmed. I am near."

Eros and his mother had already gone over the nature of the universe. Although a bit perturbed about the current motion, he was expecting this move to the next real universe. Eros's brothers and sisters were nice and fun to play with, but they didn't like to ask questions like him. So, the other pups were terrified. He concluded that knowledge helps to fight off fear, but this left him open to an awareness of other things.

"Where is Mary taking us?" Eros asked while his siblings were terrified into silence by the move.

"Ah—" Eros could sense his mother's mind hesitating. "You're too much, Eros! Wait until we get there."

Mary was none too gentle as the trip—from nowhere to somewhere—terminated with a jarring plop, but this time the box was no longer pointing at the ceiling. Tipped over, the pups could walk directly out of the box onto a hard cement floor.

"Time you got moved to the kennel," Mary stated with some finality. "Don't want you guys making messes all over my kitchen. Got chores to do, so see ya."

After Mary rearranged a small blue blanket with large ladybugs and a big dragonfly that they used for bedding, she was gone. All the puppies, even Eros, were a bit dazed, feeling they had gone through an experience when up was down and reality shifted sideways.

Curious, Eros was the first to stagger out of the box onto the open floor. The floor was as solid as a rock and as flat as the sides of their old box, but the new room was large with a chain-link fence surrounding them. Moving to the nearest wall, he found the wall to be a crisscross of heavy steel wire attached to galvanized pipes.

Above, there were pipe beams across the top with a green tarp spread across their whole ceiling. This opaque top cast a green light over the kennel, preventing the harsh sunlight from glaring on the puppies. The puppies thought this silly since they liked to bask in the sunlight, questioning the rationale of the setup. After their first rainstorm when the canvas kept them dry, they begrudgingly accepted the arrangement, but they still thought it unnecessary.

"Another box," he mused. "Like Mother said!"

This box was on the edge of the real universe, Eros concluded, though incorrectly. This effusive analysis would soon recognize that the diamond-shaped wires acted like prison bars, keeping them from another even more real reality, the Wild, or so Eros thought.

Regardless of which reality was the real reality, this reality was fascinating, and it would turn out to be more fascinating than any of the other rooms that he had explored so far, not for what was in the room but for what the puppies could see outside it.

Peering between the crisscrossing strands, Eros felt like he was in a cave, and oddly, he looked through the crisscross pattern to see another reality, one step removed from his current reality. He felt this was like seeing a reflection of firelight at the back of a cave, forming vignettes on the cave's wall.

At the farthest end of the kennel away from the door, looking through one diamond-shaped opening framed by the metal strands,

Eros could see glimpses of an object in the Wild—a gray stalk with a fluffy-topped green cap and a blue ceiling high above. The brown and green floor dominated their new vision of his universe, sprinkled with red and yellow rectangular boxes known as buildings.

The gray-green monstrosity, Eros learned, was a tree. As Eros's eyes adjusted, he started to see things beyond the tree. Since the lay of the land was flat, he perceived objects in the distance, moving back and forth beyond a large golden pasture, which Eros did not have the words to describe. (For Eros, everything in motion was a creature.)

In the future, during times when Mary would pet the pups one by one, she would place the most recently petted pup on the floor outside the box of their genesis, while she went on to pet the other puppy, giving the pups time to wander around. On one occasion, Eros came across a June bug. This horrible creature was huge *for him*, armored and with weird teeth. The bug was so intimidating that Eros gave it a wide berth.

The objects that Eros could see in the distance zipping back and forth appeared to be the same size as this beetle, but Eros had no idea that these distant beetles were much larger, since they were four-hundred yards away, partially hidden by an old farmer's stone wall and behind a thin line of trees. Obviously, this pup needed to work on his depth perception.

As Eros grew older, he discovered that the June bug was huge for him because it was close to him and he was small. These little beetles in the distance, he learned, were called cars. When they were closer, these objects would tower over him, his mother, and even Mary. On the highway partially hidden by the rock wall, the cars dashed past the farm that he was on.

The pasture itself was not noteworthy except for its beauty, blemished only by a large stone embedded in the middle of it about two hundred yards away. Eros mused that the stone looked like a big turd that he once had, only this one was gray granite. (Oddly, the puppy pack telepathically overheard this thought and playfully called the rock the Big Turd from then on.)

To the far left about two hundred yards away, a large area had been plowed, and a market garden flourished with a bounty of corn on the cob and vegetables. Beyond the garden, one could just see the top of some open construction used to sell farm products to those passing by on the roadway.

The open area of the field appeared to have been mowed recently. Beyond Eros's ken, Mary would have the hay cut down and collected over the summer and stored for feed for the livestock, but as far as Eros was concerned, either the field was growing hay or cropped.

To the right and much closer was another construction that was painted a deep red. On the left of this structure, a fenced-in area was adjacent to it. Eros could see a creature moving about in this red cedar split rail corral, but he couldn't make out what was there. Nevertheless, he did see his first birds, a couple of chickens pecking the ground between the house and the red building, which he soon learned was called a barn.

Although Skylark feared the Wild, Eros felt wonder and an instinctual urge to escape from this wire mesh cave and run loose across the brown dirt and greensward outside the kennel. He was so excited when he spied his mother that he went racing up to her, and as he did so, he blurted out breathlessly, "Mother, Mother, the Wild, it's there, yip!"

The yip stopped Eros in his tracks. That was his first yip. He was unaware that he could make any substantial sounds outside of the occasional growl as he fought the other pups for a teat. He had developed a formidable growl (at least to him it was), but this high-pitched yip didn't sound ferocious at all.

"Eros, I know!" Skylark smiled with droopy ears and her tongue hanging out. "You just barked your first bark, but it came out as a yip."

"I can make more sounds?" Eros was made aware of how little he knew about his own body. Up to now all his communications had been telepathic, except for some growling and whining when the pups were hungry, but this new sound added a different dimension to his voice that he did not expect.

(Incidentally, Eros reluctantly acknowledged that he whined, but he viewed whining as very unbecoming to his pride, so he tended to deny that he whined. He later realized that vanity led him to lie to himself.)

"Our words are few, and we separate them because most of them are what humans call exclamations." Skylark started licking Eros to his great annoyance.

"Mom," Eros complained, pulling his head away.

"Sorry, your hair was rumpled from the move." Skylark continued. "As you know, we are telepathic, but, when we get excited, we let out barks of joy, of anger, sometimes barks expressing bad words."

"How can words be bad?"

"Some words are not said in polite society. You're too young, but yes, there are bad words. And I don't want to ever hear you saying them."

"What words can I not say?"

"They're bad words, so bad that I can't repeat them!" Skylark declared.

"So I can't say certain words even though I don't know what they are yet?"

"Exactly!" Skylark nodded, while Eros was a bit confused. *Grown-ups don't make sense at times. Good thing Mother didn't hear that,* he thought.

"How will I know a word is bad if I don't know it is bad?"

"Regardless, I will scold you." Skylark assumed the mother-knows-all poise.

"Will you be scolding me because I didn't know the word was bad or because I used a bad word?"

"Tut, tut." Mother was getting annoyed with her youngling, ordering him firmly, "Back to playing with the other pups *now!*"

This was the first time Eros questioned the omniscience of his Mother. It was not the last.

Eros had trotted back to the little pack of pups when he remembered why he had approached his mother in the first place.

Being impulsive, he screeched to a halt, his four paws splayed straight out, skidding to a standstill, raising a cloud of dust. Then he reversed direction and ran back like an arrow to his mother.

"Mother, Mother, I forgot!" As Eros raced up, he said, "The Wild, it's outside the kennel. I can see it."

"Yes, you can," his mother confirmed. "But I don't want you to worry about that for now."

"Why not!" He stamped his little paw.

"You need to first learn about the Way of the dog."

"I'm ready. I'm ready," he exclaimed.

"Eros, you've only been a pup for a very short time." His mother was still miffed at him and spoke sharply. "Be a pup!"

"Why won't you tell me about the Way of the dog?"

"Because you are too young, but I will in a few weeks." Skylark's resolve hardened. "Scamper back to your siblings *now*!"

Eros recognized that tone and realized that any more questions were futile, if not dangerous. This left him in the midst of his unspoken questions, pining away for answers, and these answers seemed so desperately far away. Since Eros was less than three weeks old, a few weeks was a lifetime away.

# THE HOUSE

Over next few days, the puppies became familiar with the kennel attached to the house by a doorway that opened directly into the kitchen. During the autumn the house was always warmer at night and sometimes during the day, so the pups liked being in the house. On these occasions, Mary invited them in, especially when it was below freezing. Mary also had an ulterior motive. She liked the pitter-patter of little paws running around the house, and the puppies happily obliged.

Tumbling through the rooms one day, the puppies decided to give each room a name. There was the room off the main area where they could play when they were indoors. This room Mary called the family room, but the puppies spent so much time playing there, they called it the playroom. (Being three weeks old, they were not very creative.)

Next, there was the biggest room, which they called the main room. At times the pups also called the main room purgatory because when they were not playing and just sitting around the main room, Mary ignored them. It made them feel like they did not exist, as if they were in a no-dog-no-human land. To the sociable pups, this lack of socializing was an uncomfortable limbo, so purgatory seemed to be an appropriate name.

There was a mysterious room, which the pack called the throne room. Although there were more objects in the room, the puppies became enamored with the two closest to the door. There was a white sculpture and a huge white porcelain seat. These objects were mysterious since the doggies did not know what they were. Incomplete knowledge leads to incomplete conclusions, creating a knowledge void, which gets filled with whatever the imagination can come up with. In other words, ignorance breeds mysteriousness.

From directly below, the ceramic pew appeared to reach up to the ceiling. (From the floor it looked that way, anyway.) Mary sporadically would state to Skylark, "I'm going to hit the throne," and she would retreat to this room. Hence, their name for the room. Later the puppies would associate the name with the object people sat on.

Once, when the door was left open to the throne room, the puppy pack wandered at the foot of the great seat and got a good view of that other white edifice extending out from the wall, higher than the great throne was tall. At the time they thought these great edifices were dedicated to some mysterious force.

Later Eros learned these impressive white sculptures in the room called the bathroom had functional names. The throne was the toilet, and the projecting statue was the sink. But to the pups, these were mysterious and sacred structures, on which humans contemplated for hours on end.

Lastly, there was the beloved kitchen. This was the land of milk and meat. When the pups were weaned away from their mother, they were brought into this room and fed wonderful foods. All the cabinets that held these delights were decorated brightly with flowers of various colors. The light of the morning splashed joyfully through the windows, while Mary would put down the nectar of the gods from bags and cans.

From the bags came a spectrum of flavors in dry nuggets. From the cans came soft, juicy meat in red (beef), brown (pork), beige (chicken), and white (fish) colors. Since all the puppies thought this was the most wonderful room in the universe, excluding heaven, which they didn't know much about, they decided to call this room paradise.

There was another feature to the house that caught the puppies' attention—two staircases. The pups only got peeks at the first stairway, hidden behind a door off the kitchen. The entry was usually closed, but when it was opened, they could see it led down into a darkness below the kitchen.

The puppy pack only saw glimpses of this staircase when Mary opened the door to go down and fetch some mysterious object or other. The gloom scared the puppies, and they cringed whenever Mary went down into what they called the underworld because it was under their world.

The puppies also smelled dampness and the faint whiff of death. It was probably a long-dead mouse, but nonetheless, death was an unmistakable presence. The darkness and dampness reminded them of stories about the Big Nap, so they called the area the land before living.

The second staircase led up to what they designated as heaven, but there was a childproof gate barring their passage upstairs. Even if there was no gate, the steps leading up to heaven were so tall the puppies couldn't navigate them. Since Mary and a male friend of hers named Ted went upstairs occasionally, they figured this was a place of great happiness.

The puppy pack did have the run of the main floor of the house, excluding the throne room, but paradise was always their favorite place. Although they always yearned to see the source of happiness in heaven, paradise was unquestionably a source of joy for them on earth. This led all the puppies to question how heaven could be better than paradise. They could not understand yet.

There were two open doorways exiting the kitchen, both leading to the L-shaped main room. The larger section of the main room, where tables and chairs reigned supreme, was the living room. Mary called this an open layout floor plan, and sometimes referred to the smaller, second area of the main room as the dining room. Wrapping around paradise, the two rooms were all part of the main room, connected to the kitchen by those two doors, affording the puppies with a circular racetrack.

There was one last door that captured their curiosity. Whenever Mary left the house, she went through this door, and when she did, all the pups sat up and took notice. There was another room. It was a *big* room with a vast blue ceiling and walls with no corners and *no metal grid*. The first time they saw this door open, the puppies raced over to their mother.

"Mama, Mama," the little pack all chimed. "Is that the big room?"

"Yes, that's the Wild," Skylark responded.

"That's the same Wild we see from the kennel?"

"Yes, the humans call it New Jersey!"

"It's so big!" Wanda blurted out.

"The Wild is everywhere," Eros exclaimed in awe.

His mother wasn't sure if Eros's statement was a question or sentiment, so she left unanswered the endless question: Is it everywhere?

# THE STRANGE DOGS

**W**hile exploring the house, Eros found the bathroom door open a crack one day, not wide open but open just enough for a wee little pup to slip through. This represented an irresistible invitation for him. He squeezed through the opening without too much trouble, and he had a firsthand look at the white sculpture and the throne.

The fixtures were arranged on the right-hand side of the room. Way overhead, as if growing out of the side of the wall, a white shelf extended out with a shining silver pipe jutting out of the middle of the sculpture that plunged back into the wall. There were more details, but Eros remained focused on the sink and the drainage pipe.

After some time, he turned to the next object rising straight out of the floor. The throne was less interesting, but since it was closer, it seemed more impressive. From Eros's perspective, it was just a curved white wall. As all babies do, he licked it, trying to register a tactile sense of the object, and he also smelled what he could smell. Since the throne with the white sink appeared to be made of the same material, he categorized these items as being made of the same substance that he had just *tasted* because of the visual similarities.

Beyond this, being so high up, the sink remained a mystery, but the toilet became the enigma. *For what purpose art thou used for?* he thought, using language from a Shakespearian play that Mary had been perusing. *When Mary sat upon thee, did she become queen of the universe? Should I bow down to her at these times? For whom does this throne benefit most? Our adoration of Mary or Mary's adulation of this most holy relic?*

Eros's ignorance obviously deceived him, but after a few minutes, he decided not to worry too much about this enigma. There was too much to see to worry about what he had seen. Since he had so much more to see in the bathroom, his interest waned quickly, and off he went. The riddle of the throne would have to wait until he was bigger.

This was a country-sized bathroom, and the tub was an object d'art. Even though this was the largest thing in the room, Eros had not previously noticed the tub. Five foot long, the tub was curved on the sides, standing on four ornate stubby legs.

Jumping from object to object, some doctors would say Eros was suffering from an attention deficit hyperactivity disorder, but his attention was not deficit. Operating at a speed far above normal, Eros's hyperactivity was a reflection of the amount of information that his mind was processing, which was moving with tremendous rapidity, and not a disorder at all.

Without too much ado, Eros moved on to the largest object in the room. The white and bulbous part of the tub was raised above the floor by about a half of a foot, but Eros immediately turned his attention away from the body of the tub. The bathtub stood on small legs with feet, three of which were exposed, but Eros was fascinated by the feet facing the middle of the room.

Naturally, the foot of the tub closest to him grabbed his attention. The foot contained the face of a gargoyle, although Eros did not know what a gargoyle was. All he knew was that a grotesque face adorned this foot, and it appeared to be staring at him with unfriendly intentions.

Attempting to think like Matt, Eros approached this beast cautiously, slanting away and then doubling back. He hoped with luck that he would not be seen. From the side, he sniffed the foot and tentatively licked it, all the while the beast did not move. Gaining confidence, Eros looked directly at the foot eye to eye, and yipped a mighty yip at the beast.

Since the foot did not respond, Eros yipped at it some more until he decided that he had established his dominance over this beast. Instinctually, having demonstrated his supremacy, Eros went over and tinkled on the gargoyle face. Since Eros had consummated his dominance, he spied another foot at the other end of the tub near the back wall of the kitchen and scampered over to investigate.

After the first gargoyle, Eros's confidence had blossomed, so he was almost arrogant. Almost is the key word here. Humans can be truly arrogant, but dogs can get a bit full of themselves but never arrogant. (At least that is what dogdom tells itself.)

Nonetheless, Eros strutted over to the next foot and yipped at it a couple times right off the bat. Playing in front of the face, he demonstrated his great prowess, falling and jumping hither and thither, in and then away from the gargoyle. Remaining silent, Eros felt the monster was duly impressed.

The demonstration was so strenuous that Eros tumbled backward away from the tub. The tub was in the corner of the room, and the foot he was in the process of subjugating near the back wall continued to timidly observe him.

Eros tumbled into the open space next to the tub, parallel to both the back wall and the bathroom door. His last somersault landed him about two feet from the tub. Off-kilter when he got up, Eros was looking at the back wall. Eros had the shock of his young life. A dog was staring back at him.

"Who are you?" Eros was finally able to choke out. No response! Eros took offense at this. Every creature he had met so far was open and friendly, except the silent gargoyles, which did not count since he had easily subjugated them. With another dog, Eros interpreted this muteness as a sign of extreme hostility, and he ratcheted up his defenses as a result.

"Why don't you talk to me?" Eros took his attack stance, paws down, bum up, no wagging tail, and let out the scariest snarl he could muster. To his dismay, the strange dog took the same exact stance, silently snarling back at Eros, and it scared him!

"Yip!" Eros barked sharply. Now Eros was a tiny dog, and his yip, which sounded like a trumpet in battle to him, could hardly be heard outside the bathroom. To his dismay, Eros's yelp echoed in the bathroom, which he took to be the strange dog's first response to him. Although soft, Eros was offended by the tone of the response, to which he replied, "*Yip, yip, yip!*"

"Yip, yip, yip," came the echo.

*Bang!* The door swung sharply open, and Mary in a blue skirt and white blouse walked through brusquely. Eros was already on edge because of the gargoyles, and with the crash of the door into the wall, he leaped behind the nearest leg of the tub, the one to which he had been establishing his great prowess. Peering around his now befriended second gargoyle, Eros asked nicely if the gargoyle would be quiet for him. "Please, please, please..."

Mary walked in unaware of Eros presence. He was unable to see much of her body since he was behind the bulk of the tub that he was hiding under. Only her feet, shoes, and part of her ankles were visible to him.

Some clothing came down, which Eros had no way to identify, while Mary sat on the throne. There were strange watery gurgling sounds. Then Mary stood up, pulled up her clothing, and jiggled something to cause a huge flushing sound. She directly moved to the projecting sculpture. At the sink, more gurgling sounds occurred, and Eros thought she may be drowning. But she completed her ablutions and went quickly from the room, closing the door behind her.

Eros thanked this gargoyle for his cooperation, and out of respect, he decided not to tinkle on it. Then he realized he had a problem. When Eros had come into the bathroom, the door had been left ajar, but now it was not.

"I'm locked in." Recognizing he had a dilemma on his hands, Eros remembered with some trepidation, "I'm locked in with this hostile, strange dog!"

Eros scampered back to view the mirror on the back wall and growled at the strange dog. Before, staring back at him was one strange dog growling, but now a whole host of strange dogs peered back at him. Half had their backs to him, while the other half silently growled. Of course, mirror images don't growl, but Eros obliged. His imagination filled in the special effects, and he heard the growls that were not there.

The back wall had a full-size mirror affixed to it, which was the location of his original canine menace, but the back of the bathroom door also had a full-size mirror hanging by a wire, tilting at a slight angle. With the door closed, both mirrors faced each other, and the angles were right so that one replicated the back wall image over and over again.

Eros was now seeing himself and the reflection of himself reflected in the mirror in front of him, which was also being reflected in the mirror behind him with the reflections flicking back and forth, infinitely, while growing smaller and smaller.

"There was a strange dog," Eros talked frantically to himself. "Now strange dogs galore!"

Eros recognized a dual pattern, replicating to a far distant instance beyond his senses. He could see about eight levels into the reflections as they got smaller and smaller. This was excellent depth of vision, actually; humans could see far less, poor inferior creatures that they are. Needless to say, even though Eros could see the dualities clearly, he was most upset by the numbers of strange dogs, and he wailed.

"Maaaaaaaaaaaaaaaaaa Maaaaaaaaaaaaaaa!" Eros howled, repeating his cry! The echoes of his cries taunted him, and he blurted out a mighty, "Maaaaaaaaaaaaaaaaaa Maaaaaaaaaaaaaaa!"

"What's going on in here?" Mary burst through the door, Skylark following close behind. "What are you doing in here, Hero? Not being much of a hero it looks like!"

In keeping with her excellent rapport with dogs, Mary called Eros "Hero." For Mary, the wordplay was a little joke that amused her whenever she used it. Eros often remarked at how much humans like to say things to satisfy themselves, but how infrequently they say anything meaningful. Since Eros was short on humor at the moment, Mary's little pun did not please him.

"Maaaaaaaaaaaaaaaaaa Maaaaaaaaaaaaaaa!" he howled.

"I'm here, Eros," his mother assured him.

"There are an endless number of strange dogs here," Eros claimed, turning toward the back wall mirror. The infinite number of dogs had disappeared when the bathroom door was open, but now along with the strange dog, there was a second dog that looked exactly like his mother.

"That's a mirror!" Mother smiled at her little charge. "And that is you and me in the mirror!"

With this explanation, Skylark walked up and sat by the mirror. Eros could see that the resemblance was uncanny. His mother then licked the mirror, and the reflection followed suit, licking the mirror too.

"That's me?"

"Yes, go up and touch it," Mother assured him.

Eros complied, and as he approached the mirror, the strange dog did too. He licked the mirror, and it tasted like glass.

"It's me?"

"Yes," his mother said. "Nothing to be afraid of!"

"But what happened to the thousands of strange dogs looking at one another?" Eros complained. "Two dogs with dueling stares going on forever?"

"I don't know what you are talking about." Skylark looked around and just saw the two of them in the mirror. Eros just sounded crazy to her.

His mother had the good sense to never be caught in the bathroom with the bathroom door shut. Since Eros had been caught in the bathroom, Skylark supposed that the smarter you are, the less good sense you have. "There are no other dogs in here, Eros."

"There were!" Eros insisted.

"Don't talk nonsense." His mother lost her patience. "Out of here, scoot!"

As Eros scampered out of the room, under his telepathic breath, he said, "There were!"

# THE BOOK OF THE DOG

"**P**ups! Hmpf!" Mother harrumphed to get the attention of her underlings, which is a really funny sound coming from a dog. "Dogdom has a very ancient tome telling how the universe was created. Passed from dog to dog throughout the ages, this volume is older by many millennia than any book, including any of humanity's books. This book goes back to the beginning of time. You need to learn from *The Book of the Dog*. Let me recite to you the first chapter."

Skylark began delivering this entry as if she was reading a teleprompter.

# In the Beginning

In the beginning, there was the beginning, and from this beginning,

When everything was One, undivided, the universe was breathless,

Then this One divided and called itself God, Lord over all dualities.

God shaped this universe like a woman shaping a red clay pot.

As there was an interplay between the shape and space of the pot.

Within this hollow, an inverse image of the pot was formed,

Within which the sacred fluids of matter and life were poured,

And the form was filled with light and dark, earth and sky.

The inorganic infrastructure of the universe blossomed into reality;

The sun and the moon shone brightly on a new universe without life,

But the One was lonely, and in his loneliness he desired companionship.

The One decided to make life, a being like unto himself. God to Dog!

God created the mold from his own holy substance, and

Into his cosmic pot was poured the stuff of life: body and soul.

From this mold, two dogs were formed, Rorschach twins.

This is how the first two dogs were born. Inverse images of the One!

Although a reflection of infinity, the reflection displayed was a duality.

They were also mirror images of each other, joined at the hip.

The One designated these dogs, reverse images of her, as sublime.

God was all genders and none, but through this imperfect process,

The One shared the joy of creation with the rest of life through the sexes.

His own creativeness knew no bounds, creating for sea, land, and air.

Fish and birds, insects and salamanders, snakes and finally humans.

God got a lot of practice creating creatures, but God saw dogs' desire.

Dogs needed an assistant, but he could not get this last creation right.

Every human she created, when filled with life, also was filled with flaws.

The One kept trying until he accepted his creations imperfection,

But she set this creative impulse to be forever running, continuously.

This set the pattern of the Great Tinkerer for all her human creations.

In reality, no creation is complete but is always a work in progress.

Unlike the dog!

"God is a he, she, or the One?" Artemis blurted out. "I'm confused!"

"As you may have noticed, at times 'him' and 'her' are interchangeable for the One. Out of politeness, we don't refer to God as 'it,' although this would be technically correct and may be considered more accurate." Skylark looked over at her overwhelmed pups. "This is similar to when sometimes we don't refer to God as God or even as the One. Nouns and pronouns are profoundly unimportant in the search for the One."

This intense exchange of thoughts left the puppies exhausted, but they were impressed by their mother's memory. They would find out later, all dogs have very good memories, and a good many dogs develop eidetic memories. They also were warned that humans were never to learn of this attribute of dogs, or people would want to abuse this dogdom gift.

"That's enough for today," Mother concluded. "Mind you, during ancient times, our dog forebears tried to teach humans about creation, but they could never transcribe it right."

# PUPPIES AND PLAY

The next two weeks were filled with a lot of happiness. The five puppies tumbled over one another, playing nonstop. Their effort was fixated on growing stronger, running faster, jumping higher, and engaging the flow of change within their bodies. They easily exceeded the Losada line without even trying.

The puppies didn't realize that they were getting bigger. They figured the things that they thought were large were getting smaller. Over the days, their perception of objects adjusted. The puppies' openness meant that they welcomed the change within every object, from their Being to just Be. Imagine the joy if all dogs and people were as open!

Charley was a tough little pup, using his superior strength to his advantage, but he didn't understand leverage. Now and again, he would bowl Eros over. In other instances, Eros would use Charley's momentum to keep rolling, throwing Charley off. The two of them had great little battles. Eros loved it when Charley snorted because he knew the battle was not going according to Charley's liking.

"That's not fair," Charley would say, snuffling. "Snort! Snort! You need to stand and fight."

"If I did, I'd lose," Eros replied. "Then it wouldn't be fun to fight."

"It would be for me," Charley declared.

"But it wouldn't be for me," Eros replied.

Charley pondered what Eros had said, and over the ensuing couple of days, he changed. Eros gave Charley more respect for this effort at changing himself, far more than Eros ever did for Charley's strength. Change is hard to do! Also, Charley demonstrated that he was not a dumb dog. He never brought up the "fight like a dog" argument again, but he did continue to snort when the battle was not going well to Eros's great amusement.

After this exchange, their battles were different. They were more fun! Occasionally, when Eros was not having a good day, he felt Charley let him win, but he could not be sure. There was more to Charley than his brute strength, and all of the pups thought he was destined to become the leader of a pack.

Artemis was the most docile of the litter. She was pleasant and played with the other pups at times, especially when the puppies all jumped into the fray. Mostly she liked being with their mother and learning the mysteries of motherhood. To Artemis, this was what life was all about, the producing of new life, and she was thrilled to have this responsibility.

In her way, Artemis was the smartest of the litter because her simple approach to life gave her a vision that extended beyond today. Eros knew he was clever and had a great curiosity, but he was not smart like Artemis, a true visionary of what was to be and how to be ready for it. Because they didn't have common interests to start, the two talked infrequently during the first few weeks.

Matt was the trickster. He loved to go one way, and when a puppy was turned away, he would spin around and jump onto his victim's back. Matt, the prankster, liked it when his opponents were unaware of his approach and were most vulnerable. While Charley's strength and directness were easy to deal with, in contrast, Matt's cunning attacks often found Eros at a disadvantage. These bouts were hard to counteract, and the play tended not to be fun. Although Charlie would shrug Matt off like he would a fly, Eros was not strong enough to do this to his sneaky sibling, so he learned a rule: *Don't turn your back unless you know what is there.*

"Submit!" Matt rushed from the side, hoping it was Eros's blind side.

"Never!" Eros chivalrously replied, pretending to be the gallant green dog who fought all his battles with honesty and bravery and a strict set of rules of engagement.

With Eros's declaration, the two of them went at it with more fervor, tussling and turning, leaping and growling as much as the little puppies could growl. During this clash, Matt caught a fold of Eros's fur in his teeth and bit hard.

"Owww!" Eros yipped, and he squirmed violently, pulling himself free. *"That hurt!"*

Then Eros looked down, and he was bleeding, red blood streaking down his golden fur onto the floor. This wasn't a gusher, but enough blood flowed to startle Eros.

"That's what this is all about," Matt crooned like he had won the victory of all victories, as if he knew what 'this' was.

Eros ran off to their mother. She listened to his complaints. Nevertheless, she had no criticism of Matt. Skylark calmed him down and licked his wound until it stopped bleeding, but all she would say was that it was the Way of the dog. From that point on, Eros was hard-pressed to trust Matt. Turning his back on Matt in the future became a strategic decision.

Wanda was Eros's favorite. She was Artemis and Charley in one dog. She was docile some of the time, but she would be playful like Charley a lot too. In fact, where Charley was so direct and became predictable and boring, Wanda was more variable, attacking from different angles and twisting in ways Charley couldn't even imagine. Her constant chatter accompanying their play made it really, really fun.

"Ho, I've got you now," Wanda crowed.

"No, you don't," Eros parlayed, flipping her over.

"Yes, well," Wanda groaned as she exerted leverage to shift his energy in a different direction. "*Now* I do!"

The conversation was not intellectually stimulating, but the ongoing chitchat helped both to hone their telepathic skills while in the midst of action.

Even the feel between Wanda and Charley was different. Where Charley was developing a lot of muscles, Wanda was strong but soft. She would wrap around Eros, and he felt a happiness in her touch. This was not sexual. Eros did not know what sex was at this time, and he had no sexual urges yet. He guessed that he just liked females. Because of his ignorance of his own body, he didn't know why.

The greatest fun was when all five of the pups conspired, hiding their telepathic thoughts, and together, they came up with plans to pounce on their mother all at once. All the while, Mother would pretend to not know that the puppy pack was coming. (The puppy pack's telepathic control was not perfect. Charley was especially transparent, so Skylark always knew.)

After a few minutes of scheming, the five of them would agree to have Artemis and Matt sneak up from one direction, while Wanda, Charley, and Eros would pretend to be playing, creating a diversion for the twosome to approach their mother from another direction, undetected. Then from Skylark's blind side, Artemis and Matt would *pounce*! As quickly as possible, Wanda, Charley, and Eros would follow suit.

On one occasion, their jumps were timed perfectly, or as perfect as puppies could be, as they all leaped into the air as one and pounced synchronously. This particular instance was the only time Skylark was truly surprised since near perfection is a rare commodity.

This period contained some of the most memorable and fun moments of their lives. There were no worries. Food and a warm dwelling were provided, and they had plenty of time to mindlessly play. They happily embraced the delusion that this experience would last forever. Later Eros would rationalize that they were developing muscles and tactics to maximize their potential for survival in the future, but learning could not have been more fun.

As the pups grew older, their play became fiercer, and jumping on their mother was less frequent because they could no longer coordinate their actions. As normal, the puppies evolved into five pups moving in different directions, and they began their journey into the *terrible twos*. (For humans, this refers to two-year-olds, but for dogs, it refers to two-month-olds.) They were five puppies, pulling the same toy in different directions, so working together became impossible.

Even in paradise, on their sixth-week birthday, they had to be separated now and again as two pups sought for the same chunk of meat. This is where they learned to snarl loudly. Eros was surprised when hunger caused a lust for food that made poor little puppies do regrettable things, including himself.

Regardless, these were some of the happiest days of Eros's puppyhood, and they were the memories that were the easiest to lose when these days came to an end.

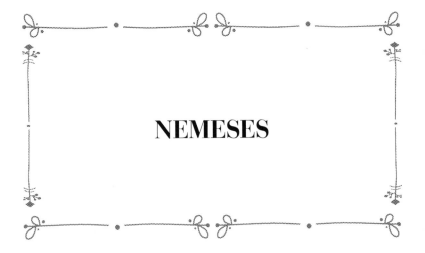

# NEMESES

The puppies learned that the house had two disturbing dangers that sent them scrambling to get into the kennel or hide if the kennel door was not open. Every other day, this metal and plastic beast would emerge from a closet and roar to life with a glaring light, searching for them. Relentlessly, this monster would run around the house, terrorizing poor wee doggies.

Eros, as well as the other pups, could only envision the worst. If they were not fast enough, this postindustrial brute would run right over them, chew them up, and suck them into its glassy innards. They imagined blood and guts spurting everywhere inside the monster's see-through stomach, completing a gruesome fantasy. Fear could create some nasty fantasies, and this was one of them. From Mary, they learned that the beast was called a vacuum cleaner.

The pattern of this visitation was repeated over and over. From nowhere (at least to the oblivious pups), the vacuum cleaner would appear, grumbling and growling. To the sound of a roaring wind, five pups would jump in five different directions. They never really saw that Mary was pushing the mechanical creature. All they focused on was the monstrous head of the beast with two beady bright lights for eyes.

Young animals like puppies have great imaginations that are commensurate with their species. Dogs being the smartest beings on earth, this naturally corresponds to the greatest imagination. (Don't you wish you had such a great imagination, but then again, would you?)

As the vacuum cleaner started to move, Eros could see its face and hear it snarling and growling, leaping forward to try to snare one of the poor puppies in its grasping maw! Backing away violently, the metal beast would retreat as if coiling up like a snake, ready to strike again.

The already scattered pups would one by one race to the kennel door only to find it closed and not available for escape. Every time, the vacuum cleaner would presciently follow them, and they would scamper off in different directions. (In hindsight, Eros wondered if this was the way Mary planned this activity, but he could not believe she would purposely torture her puppies.)

Circling around the beast, the puppies would head for the couch because in their experience this monster was always floor-bound. On the couch, they could hide in plain sight. Without fail, the puppies found themselves perched above the fray, huddling as the mechanical creature went back and forth below them, bellowing for the puppies to face its wrath.

Eventually, the mighty monster would give up searching for puppy flesh. One by one, Eros leading the way, they would peer over the edge of the couch until there were five puppy heads. As one they would look to the right and the left, back and forth for several minutes. Breaking the spell, Eros, the courageous one, would leave the little brigade and leap off the couch. The rest of the puppies soon followed. Acting as scouts, the pack searched every room, confirming that the beast had withdrawn from battle.

The puppies surmised that the vacuum cleaner must have sucked in a mouse or a bunch of insects and having satisfied its hunger, the roaring beast had departed from the house.

There was a second danger in the house, but this was thrust upon them by their most trusted human, Mary. This entailed the very dangerous activity of grooming, namely cutting the puppy's hair and trimming their claws. Miniature poodles do not shed like other dogs. Their hair just grows and grows, so it needs to be cut, but as far as the puppies cared, let it grow!

It amused Eros, in particular, when he imagined himself as a huge ball of fur with six-inch talons for claws, rolling down a hill and doing play battles. The fur would protect him from every bite, and his unclipped claws could inflict indescribable damage. He would be invincible! (He did not dwell much on the fact that getting around and eating may be a bit more difficult.)

When the puppies were around two and a half months, Mary pulled out a miniature machine that was as terrifying as the vacuum cleaner, only much smaller. Mary could hold this unit in her hand, and it buzzed and hissed like a bee or snake. She called this machine the clippers. (This first grooming was late, but Mary held off because she loved it when the pups became little hairballs with faces sticking out.)

Eros remembered the first time he went through this ordeal. One by one, Mary sought out a pup. When a victim was found, she subjected him or her to this torture. Eros was the best at hiding, and he hid under the couch with his eyes closed, confident that he would never be found.

Charley, being so good, was at the front of the line. Nevertheless, he grunted and whimpered often throughout the ordeal, once crying when Mary accidentally nicked him. Wanda complained nonstop to whoever would listen at the indignity of this procedure, but to no avail. Artemis got nicked and howled, but that was not her fault. It hurt. As Matt was pulled into the lap of this torturer, he whined and cried like a little baby pup not finding his mother, and he did not let up throughout his grooming.

"Hero!" Mary called. Finally, it was Eros's turn, and he could not help but open his eyes to the puppy horror movie about to unfold.

"That's where you have got to, Hero!" Peering under the couch, Mary swiftly reached in to grab the startled puppy. "Can't hide from me, you little bugger!"

Off he was, dragged by the executioner in a pink dress. Not dwelling on his failure at hiding, Eros put on a stern face and did not whine or complain. Even so, he did not hesitate to put forth his views through rational criticism for all the good it did him. Wanda stated later that it sure sounded like complaining.

"Dogs are too proud to fear humiliation," was a maxim circulating among dogdom, and that fortified his courage.

Courage is such a vulnerable concept. Sometimes a soldier does things and does not know they are courageous until after he has done them. No one truly knows what has guided them to perform a courageous act. Once in the flow of an engagement, labels like courage or cowardice fade in contrast to the primal urges of fight or flight.

Was it pride or fear or duty or the illusion that he or she was invulnerable (a common delusion of the young) that produced valor? There are a thousand emotional currents that can support an individual on the island of courage. Eros was relying on his pride in this instance, yet he felt that pride was a weak foundation for bravery.

Funny how fast pride can dissipate as Eros was taken to a table and thrown on his back. Then the clippers cut a swath up the side of his belly. In his panic, he was imagining his belly sliced open and his guts spewed across the table, while Mary was laughing maniacally. That was definitely a grisly mental image!

Eros remained silent simply because he was too stunned to make any sound. After finishing his stomach and chest, Mary flipped him right side up and passed the clippers back and forth across his back. After a few swipes, his fear kept telling him to scream at this intrusion into the sanctity of his body, but his back started telling him that he liked the transiting clippers as if he were being given a unique massage.

Mary focused on his head and turned lastly to his face. This was when fear returned with a vengeance as Eros could see the small beast, its teeth churning back and forth at super speed. During the pass across his face, Mary held Eros fast, moving the clippers around his eyes with great skill. At the time, Eros did not appreciate Mary, but later his estimation of Mary's skill at grooming rose as he passed through subsequent groomers in the years to come.

The last part of this torturous path was the clipping of his claws. Eros saw these huge scissor-like clippers with two talons nearly colliding together. To his horror, this abomination was approaching his own claws. In hindsight, he thought that if he were a human, this would be like using hedge shears to trim a fingernail.

Once Mary nicked the quick of one of his claws, and Eros stifled the cry, not because he was courageous, but because he choked on the sound he was going to make. Fortunately, this was the last claw, and Mary put him down immediately, further distracting him from the pain.

"Oh, that was so brave!" Wanda praised him, eyeing him as if he were a god. "You are the only pup that didn't make a sound, and look, you are bleeding!"

The claw that had been nicked was showing some blood, which Eros began licking, but this red badge of courage matched his involuntary silence through the ordeal and sealed his reputation, which followed him wherever he went.

*Am I courageous?* Eros wondered. This was a question that he was unable to answer as he pondered his nemeses, the vacuum cleaner and the clippers. *Or lucky?*

# IN THE WILD, SORT OF

E ros had grown to be tall and lean over the last eleven weeks, eating voraciously and growing as his appetite grew. He was almost as tall as his mother on a good day, about a foot, and had packed on almost nine pounds of lean muscle. He could match Matt's play, which was beyond the edge of being playful, but neither of the pups came anywhere near Charley's strength.

Having a few extra pounds on Matt and Eros, Charley could fend off both of them and bounce them to the end of the kennel if he chose to do so. From his early play lessons with Eros, Charley just elected to go forward by maintaining the "fun for all and not just for himself" policy. In a way, Charley was still the gallant green dog reincarnated and Eros had to admit he himself was not. (Regardless of this awareness, Eros continued to aspire to be gallant.)

During the day, the pups were left mainly in the kennel, but at night and in the early morning, they came into the house to feed in paradise. Before the pups were housebroken, only for a short time at night were they allowed to wander about the house under Mary's tight supervision after dinner.

During these forays, Skylark and Artemis and occasionally Wanda would sit together, talking about having pups and how to bring puppies up, while the rest of Skylark's current litter would run in circles around the house.

Mary let this go on for a while, but if they got too rambunctious, after about twenty minutes, she either yelled at the pups to slow down or kicked them out, sending them back to the kennel. When this exile because of bad behavior happened, Mary allowed the females, who had not partaken in the roughhousing, to stay in. (Wanda often got the boot!)

Charley, Matt, Eros, and sometimes Wanda, who was banished on this particular night, continued running in circles in the kennel. Eros was practicing his jumping, bouncing against the chain-link fence. What one dog learns the rest will too. This batch of puppies all became jumpers to a degree, but Eros was superior at this skill.

As Mary watched, it became apparent to her that the kennel was getting too small for the pups.

"Crowded in there, getting to be like the pigsty," Mary mused to herself. Skylark heard her and became uneasy.

"Okay, Shyla," Mary roused Skylark the next morning from her slumbers. "Today we take these scalawags outside."

"No," Skylark telegraphed to Mary, but as usual, Mary could not listen very well, which seemed to be a particularly strong human trait.

"Yep, those rascals are tearing up the place," Mary continued, oblivious that she was having a conversation with Skylark. Mary reacted as if she was hard of hearing, perceiving only pieces of the conversation, and unbeknownst to her, she was.

"They are not ready!" Skylark pleaded.

"Sure enough, they're ready!" Mary disagreed. "Heck! Hero is jumping halfway up the side of the kennel, almost four feet!"

Each dog had developed individual traits that were superior to the other pups' traits. Charley grew stronger. Matt grew more cunning. Artemis saw all of their futures better than any of the puppies, and Wanda developed a sense of sarcasm that was usually humorous.

Outside of his metaphysical bent, Eros developed a superior ability to jump. He started this skill when Mary would come out to give scraps to the pups from her table. By definition, these leftovers were marvelous, but they usually went down so fast, the pups never tasted them. Mary tossed the morsels to the puppy pack, but the bits were gobbled up so quickly that they never hit the ground.

Because of this, the pups would frantically gather around Mary, leaving no room for Eros. To get her attention, Eros would jump at the back of the pack. Mary found this amusing and rewarded him by throwing a scrap high in the air. And from that moment on, he jumped all the time, and Mary made sure to reward him.

Eros soon found jumping against the side of the kennel gave him an advantage in their puppy play battles as he could get away from any pup chasing him, even Charley, and if he timed it right, Eros could run straight up the side of the kennel and come back down on top of his chaser, making the chaser the chasee.

"Mary, please, not yet," Skylark begged.

"Now I know you think they are not ready," Mary prattled on, oblivious to the fact that she was in a conversation. "But I think they are, and we will be standing there watching them, you and me!"

With that, Mary went off to the kennel, called the pups out, and walked them to the door leading to the Wild. Skylark was jumping around, very anxiously trying to tell Mary, "Stop this insanity!" Mary was insensible to Skylark's pleas and let the puppies loose without a second thought.

All of the pups were wide-eyed and in awe at how big this big room was. The puppies had seen the sky, earth, trees, and buildings when the house door had been opened on occasion, but this was *big*. This experience was so unlike looking through the little diamond-shaped chinks in the fence presenting revelatory visions in small vignettes.

This landscape was not small and limited. All their eyes had developed just as their mother foretold, and outside this door, the Wild presented a panorama far beyond their expectations. Over the weeks, the pups' eyesight had improved immensely, so much so that Eros could see a mouse skitter across the top of the Big Turd two hundred yards away, but this vast reality went beyond the limits of their vision.

Looking up, the puppy pack marveled at the white fluffy blobs framed by an endless, bright blue sky when they realized that these fluffy marvels were moving. Looking through the chinks in the fence, they had not noticed the detail of movement. They had always rationalized motions outside in the Wild as caused by the movement of their muzzle or tricks of the mind.

Admittedly, staying put and watching a cloud move did not rank highly as a pastime in the puppies' nonstop kennel play, so a moving muzzle or mental foible was as good a rationale as any at that time.

"Clouds. Those are clouds," Skylark announced, explaining what the white blobs were. "You must beware of clouds because they hide the beasts of the wind, birds that want to eat little puppies!"

"Oh, *Mother!*" the pups scoffed in unison. Over and over, Skylark repeated her warnings with the voice of doom, and as usual, her charges duly ignored her and wandered off.

"Charley," Eros exclaimed as he watched his brother generally looking downward, "isn't the sky beautiful and blue? Look up!"

"Eros, I focus on the here and now," Charley responded matter-of-factly.

"That cloud there looks like a dog bone." Eros amused himself, associating shapes with objects that he was familiar with. Being metaphysical, this was more in line with Eros's idea of play rather than Charley's.

"Everything happens down here, not in the sky!" Charley insisted. "You have to use your eyes to look around but your nose to see. That way nothing can ever sneak up on you. Clouds are for dreamers."

"Am I a dreamer?"

"Yes!" His mother interjected with a telepathic smile, having intercepted their conversation. "You dream of the existence beyond the eyes of all. You dream of being in the eye of the universe. From high to low, we all desire to be dreamers, but you dream most of all."

"You are Eros, the metaphysical dog!" Charley smiled. Somehow, somewhere, this appellation for Eros had arisen as a nickname of affection, even respect.

Letting their noses lead the way, all of the pups proceeded to explore. One would think with their excellent eyesight that puppy noses would not be very useful, but though their eyesight was maybe three times better than most humans, their noses were a hundred times better.

In contrast, the human's sense of taste was a hundred times better than the dog's, but for dogs, this was an inconsequential advantage. In fact, as far as a dog was concerned, this was another human deficit. If survival comes down to eating a nice gob of goop, a human may choke, unable to eat it, while a dog would easily scarf it down. Survival comes first, and if you can't eat, you can't survive. A dog's logic is impeccable, or so they think.

In a similar line of thought, a human's olfactory sense is extraordinarily deficient. Where a human would gag on an obnoxious smell, any one of the pups would sniff a complex world of aromas interwoven together. A dog would inhale a smell as if it were a bouquet with many flavors, while a human would perceive that combined odor as loathsome.

Having a superior ability to manage smells, dogs could put aside the abhorrent aspect of an odor like setting a sugar bowl on a shelf, while they could explore the rest of the smells hidden below the surface. The most obnoxious smells were the most complex and mesmerizing.

Since the world was filled with such a wonderful variety of scents, a dog's greatest distraction for achieving a pure state of mind was not in bodily urges such as sex but rather the distracting smells of the world.

When dropped in the barnyard by Mary, the pups went off in five directions, eyes firmly fixed on the brown dirt of the yard, noses down, and scents galore entering their olfactory universe. Some of the scents were interesting or boring. Dirt is dirt after all. But some scents were so intriguing that they were enthralled. Today, all scents were new, even the boring ones!

The puppies roamed in different directions. Matt wandered in circles so much that he ended up chasing his tale, but Eros wandered the farthest and came to short green stalks sprouting out of the dirt. Eros took a long time smelling these living plants, the first he had ever known.

(Mary raised dogs only. No plants were allowed indoors. Mary would complain that after taking care of the farm animals she spends all her waking hours tending to the plants in the market garden and would not consider keeping an ornamental plant in the house. "Plants ain't ornaments!" she would say.)

"That's called grass," Mother continued.

Not far away, searching among the patches of grass for worms, two chickens strutted and pecked. The first was saying, "Got to find the worm," while the second was mindlessly poking at the ground.

"Hi!" Eros was thrilled to speak with anything other than dogs. (He couldn't say that he really talked with Mary. She just talked at him.)

"All animals have some telepathy," Mary thoughtfully inserted an answer before the question about whether other animals had telepathy formed.

"Whatchya doing?" Eros continued seamlessly with a slight mental nod of thanks, acknowledging his mother's insight.

"Got to find the worm!" the first chicken seemed to reply. Eros was not sure if this comment was directed at him or not.

"My name is Eros. What is yours?" Eros was uncertain if the conversation had begun, but he continued as if it had.

"Name? No name! Squawk! What name?" The first chicken looked at her companion. "Do you have a name?"

"Peck, Squawk, Peck, Squawk!" the second replied.

"If you're Squawk, I must be Peck, right?" the first chicken questioned. She was obviously the scholar among these two chickens. Later Eros discovered she was the Einstein among all the chickens in the barnyard.

"Squawk, Peck!" the second chicken confirmed.

"Eros..." His mother watched this exchange with some amusement. "Chickens aren't too bright."

"Got to find the worm! Squawk!" The first chicken went back to her ruminations while pecking the ground when it suited her. There were no worms in sight, but this pecking trait was an insatiable nervous habit for these birds, as Eros soon learned a thousand pecks gets the worm.

"This grass is boring." Eros blamed the grass for his disappointment that the chickens were not worthy conversationalists. "Nothing happens here in the grass!"

"You must beware of grass!" His mother repeated her relentless mantra about fearing things in the Wild. "The grass hides the beasts of the earth—venomous snakes and insects that want to eat little puppies!"

Eros, as expected, rolled his eyes and shrugged his shoulders, learning a bit of the art of not listening. Fortunately, due to Eros's nature of asking questions, the bad habit of not listening could not last, but for some, it lasts a lifetime.

With Skylark's traditional doomsday declaration, she shooed Eros back to the house. When he looked up, he couldn't believe that they had gotten almost fifty yards away. With a smile, Eros leaped at the challenge and ran headlong back to the house with occasional leaps that made him feel he was jumping to the top of the sky.

His mother wasn't in the mood to race, but nonetheless, she was impressed by her pup's fifty-yard sprint.

Eros rushed up to the door of the house with a mighty bound. Standing on the raised steps before the door, he turned around and looked over the rest of the pups, the barnyard, and beyond. Eros spied the red barn, and he was tempted to try his newfound running ability in that direction when his mother stepped in his way.

"*No*," she spoke sternly as only a mother can, hard steel in her telepathic voice, projecting emphatic finality. "You do not go to the barn."

"I see creatures there and lots of new smells." Eros was a soon-to-be teenager (by weeks, not years), and as typical, he questioned every boundary that his mother wouldn't let him check out.

"Those are the inferior creatures of the earth," Skylark informed all the pups. "On the list of holy priorities, there are first dogs, humans, and then the inferior creatures of the earth and the air. Humans are stupid, but inferior creatures can be either cleverer or dumber than humans. The clever ones want to eat you or boss you around, and the dumb ones don't know better and will step on you. Both can and will kill you. Beware of all creatures that are not dogs!"

"You make the Wild sound scary," Wanda piped up. "But all we have had is the most fun of our lives!"

"There is order, and there is chaos!" Mother informed her. "Chaos might seem like fun, but order means safety. The Wild puts on a placid face, but underneath lie vipers and scorpions and birds of prey. I will say this over and over. Beware of the Wild!"

Of course, over and over again, her puppies duly ignored her.

# WANDA

On one of the following days, the puppies lolled around in the barnyard. At first, they sniffed and smelled, but no new odors piqued their interest. Among the chickens crisscrossing the yard, pecking for any leftover kernels of corn, the puppies wandered around or played, but this was not a big exploration day. Wanda and Eros decided to play.

Wanda frolicked, romping to the right and back to the left. Front paws going up and down, she was like a little unicorn pirouetting deep in a forest. Obviously, she was not a unicorn, and the forest was in their imagination; however, Wanda and Eros were embraced by this magical moment as they danced in the dust that they were kicking up. Shortly, the dance ended as they stopped to confront each other squarely and take a breather.

"Beat those fancy moves," Wanda declared.

During this face-off, Eros stood in his "I want to play" position, bum up, two front paws down, his nose in between his paws, and his tail wagging furiously. When Wanda requested accolades, Eros launched himself, and the two of them rolled around in a spherically shaped living ball, back and forth, in the middle of the barnyard. Eventually, the doggie ball fell apart, and the two of them splayed themselves across the brown sward, exhausted.

"I saw something, but you won't believe me!" Eros tentatively started a discussion after shaking off the dust as the two of them exited the flow.

"You think I'm dumb? Dumb as a human?" Wanda quipped. The expression about humans being less than smart was a common derogatory reference in dogdom society. The human phrase equivalent is "thick as a plank" or its derivative, "thick as a brick," which in doggie history, originated not as a comment of humanity's lack of intelligence but from the human's thick barricade against receiving telepathic thoughts.

"No," Eros replied quickly. "I think you are really, really smart, but even Mother didn't believe me."

"Well, that's better!" Wanda smirked. "What is this great secret of yours?"

"I found a mirror in the bathroom," Eros instructed. "Have you ever looked in a mirror?"

"No," Wanda admitted. "But mirrors are no secret."

"A mirror is a glass wall in which you can see yourself." Eros felt his explanation needed some work, but it sufficed for now. Although Eros could accept that when facing directly on, the dog in the mirror was him, he still could not associate the multiple dogs as duplicate images of himself. "And I could see two dogs, staring at each other, one with its back to me. Suddenly, I could see more dogs in the same poses...and then more and more going on forever—at least as far into forever that I could see."

"Two dogs? Twins? Dual partners in infinity?" Wanda playfully surmised. "I wonder if they were friends."

"I don't know," Eros responded, irked that Wanda was not more awestruck at his story and frustrated that he could not yet transfer telegraphic images to Wanda since his mingling skills were not advanced enough. He had to admit, "The muzzles that I could see displayed more surprise than anything else."

"Maybe you did see infinity?" Wanda joked.

"I don't know what that is. I can't even imagine infinity." Eros didn't catch Wanda's shrewd levity.

"My, my, two dogs going on forever? Were they a male and a female?" Wanda was just playing with Eros now. "That's a classic duality!"

"I don't know." Eros was getting dismayed at his lack of knowledge.

"Is that the first ever duality?" Wanda hypothesized.

"The first?"

"The first duality before all dualities?" Wanda was clever at twisting scenarios all around. "The prime duality?"

"No!" Peck the chicken blurted out. "No, chicken! No, egg! Squawk! Chicken, egg!"

"Stupid chicken." Eros ignored the wisdom of the feathered nitwit, ironically ignoring the chicken's contribution to the conversation. "I don't understand, Wanda. The first what?"

"You don't know much," Wanda declared. "Mother would say you were a wise dog for admitting your ignorance."

"I can't see how I am wise."

"Ah, how about the first cause?" Wanda cried. "What caused the first duality? Or did the first duality cause the first cause?"

Eros had been beaten into silence. He resisted further admitting his ignorance, reluctant to make himself wiser than he already was. Wanda had out-questioned the dog of many questions. The infinite number of dualities had spawned an infinite number of questions and a limited number of answers.

He could only agree with her logic, which irked him to no end. Eros hesitantly confessed, "I don't know."

"For all the questions you ask, you don't have many answers," Wanda concluded triumphantly. "At this rate, you have to be the wisest dog at Farmdale."

# THE WAY OF THE DOG

S hortly after the puppy pack was transferred to the Wild (sort of), Mother sat them all down to talk. Before her, the litter was splayed across a dark blue rug in the main room, sitting in different positions. Basically, they were lolling about after a hearty dinner. Since moving to the kennel, the pups were less active when they were in the house.

Artemis looked like she was sleeping, but her sharp telepathic skills allowed her to listen all the time, even asleep, a helpful trait for a prospective mother with new pups. Eros felt this attribute contributed to her visionary nature since she was always learning.

Eros always felt Artemis knew more about the universe instinctively, while he had to resort to questions. She had a sense about how the next few weeks would unfold, which was uncanny, while he had to piece together ideas and projections to form a guess of the future.

For him, the future was filled with potential and possibilities. For Artemis, these concepts were moving and forming patterns, which Eros could not see. Eros doubted she knew the future, but he also doubted his own knowledge because she always seemed to know better.

While Charley sat at attention, listening diligently to his mother's every word, he didn't always understand all that he was hearing. While the title *intellectual* would be a stretch for him, Charley was no dummy. He was a devoted pragmatist.

Smirking off on the side, Matt always seemed to be on one side or the other, waiting to perform a sneak attack. For Mother, Matt accepted a temporary truce, but old habits tend to linger, and Eros could not relax unless Matt was in front of him.

Wanda was flopping, her body splayed in all directions, eyes wide open. She was in a constant state of stretching as if bored. Paradoxically, she was fully alert. Watching Wanda and thinking how obvious she pretended to not be interested, Eros just sat with his head cocked slightly to the side, curious as always, waiting for the show to start.

"Children, listen up!" Mother spoke with a piercing tone of thought. All the pups perked up, even the indolent appearing Wanda twitched.

"I want your attention," Skylark looked at each pup in turn to make sure they were listening to her, feeling their puppy telepathic connections lock in with hers. "Beyond the house and the kennel, there is the Wild. The Wild may not seem dangerous. Nevertheless, there is danger lurking everywhere. Always be aware in the Wild. You will soon be let out in the Wild every day, and I won't always be there to watch you. You've heard this many times before, but *always* beware of the Wild."

"Okay, *Mama*." The pups tuned out their mother temporarily because of her boring doomsday repetitiveness. Skylark paused to let this message sink in when in reality it was dribbling off.

"Now," she barked, sharply. Their mother was well aware of her pup's lagging attention span when she brought up the danger of the Wild. "I have to tell you about the Way of the dog." she continued.

"The Way?" Wanda chirped.

"Yes, children, the Way of the dog." Mother looked them over with an intense stare, which quieted their shuffling and stretching to a grinding silence.

"Why do you say Way and not the way?" Eros noted the difference. "You've done so before."

"The Way is the Way of all ways," his mother cryptically replied. "And the Way of the dog is the Way of all Ways!"

Eros decided not to venture further into Skylark's pretentiously enigmatic explanation. He was not sure he knew a way to do so.

"The Way of the dog is to understand that life is hard, but our mandate is to survive no matter how hopeless and to always seek the joy embedded in happiness wherever and whenever we can." Skylark checked in on the puppies' attentiveness and found that the not-listening malaise had dissipated and the puppies were fully alert.

"Life can be downright difficult." She continued. "We will not be together for much longer. With the humans, we come, but then we will be going. A dog's life is transient. We are born, and we will die as all creatures are destined to do. In the meantime, most of you will find lives elsewhere."

"What is die?" Eros piped up naturally.

"No questions!" Skylark answered sharply but not just to Eros— although she did ratchet up the intensity of her stare in his direction until he felt like he was a pup on his first day after the Big Nap. More softly, she added, "Later..."

"If life is good," Mother resumed, "you'll have a wonderful twelve weeks, maybe more, of puppyhood to romp and play and tussle with your siblings. We have been following a good flow within nature, but this period of time is about to end. One day one of you will be gone, but inevitably another will be next. With luck, all will be gone. You will find new homes and new humans. You must teach the humans to be good to you, and if they are receptive, you can teach them how the universe can be good to them.

"Some of you will find good humans, some not so good. This is life among the humans. Many humans will cherish you like Mary, but some become a beast of the Wild and beat you, while others will abandon you to the Wild." Mother scanned across her brood with a knowing look. "The Wild can be deceiving, and humans most of all. Much of the time, the Wild is deceptively mild. Nevertheless, danger always lurks."

"Most humans are not honest with themselves. At least the human who beats you is honest about how he feels about you. Beaters don't need to pretend to have reasons. Most don't know why they're beating you. But at least they know they don't love you, and they are telling you so when they beat you."

"Oh, that's terrible," Artemis blurted out. Then she realized she was supposed to be silent. "Sorry!"

"A human who beats you cannot love. For whatever reason, they are so angry that their anger is all they know. There is no room for love." Skylark paused.

"Abandoners are different," Mother said and sniffed, holding back some tears. Through mingling, it was clear that she had once been loved and abandoned. "An abandoner has no idea how he or she feels. These are the most dishonest people. My first owner abandoned me!"

As if dealing with the grief of losing a loved one all over again, Skylark stopped her explanation and embraced a stoic calm as best she could. She paused for a few seconds. Emotions from her past welled up, and she took time to compose herself before continuing.

She recalled to the puppies how she truly loved her first owner, and she knew that he had loved her; however, soon after she lost her puppy cuteness, her first owner hid his love for her from himself. Although she attempted to shield her puppies from her feelings, Skylark didn't know if her pups received these deep emotional thoughts. She assumed only partial success, since mingling is not conducive to hiding emotions.

"You must forgive humans. It is not their fault that they know not what they do. They are stupid creatures. That my munchkins comes from *The Book of the Dog*, but I digress." Mother rallied and pressed on. "Humans don't realize that when they obtain the companionship of a dog, it is a lifelong commitment for both the dog *and* that person. They also don't realize that in seeking to have a dog, humans are seeking love, and the dog will love their owner. But the human has to learn how to love the dog back before he can learn how love works."

"You have to learn how to love back before you can learn how to love," Artemis clarified by repeating what she thought she had heard.

"Yes," her mother confirmed.

"Are humans really that stupid that they resist learning about love?" Artemis was astounded.

"Yes, dogs try to teach the owners love, and we do our best. But many don't or won't listen. This just demonstrates the depth to which humanity's depravity can descend!"

"So stupidity is not listening to our advice?" Eros questioned, but he had little hope for an answer.

"If the owner won't listen to our wisdom, what happens?" Charley asked.

"It's not a matter of won't; they can't love," Skylark summarized. "Bad owners become subliminally aware that they can't love anything else, man or beast. This makes the owner angry or forces them into a state of denial—and you embody what they are angry at or what they are denying."

*Subliminal awareness?* Eros pondered, concluding it must be something he was not yet made aware of.

"I'm trying to think like a human," Wanda considered sarcastically. "You know the love you feel exists yet you insist on ignoring it? How can you ignore love?"

"To ignore is knowing something that you do not want to know, which you conclude does not exist, even though you know it does." Her mother replied. "And the verb 'to ignore' is at the heart of ignorance. Ignorance is a common affliction among humans!"

For puppies, this information was very interesting. This knowledge prepared them to survive their future owner, if said owner was less than a sterling example of humanity.

Skylark's puppies were entranced by her presentation as demonstrated by a mild tension coursing through all their bodies. Wanda pretended to the others that she was relaxed, stretching for minutes on end, but she was tightly wound and would have jumped if a butterfly had touched her.

Conversely, Eros was squirming with many questions, a bubble in the sun waiting to burst. These two were not alone as the other pups were similarly engaged, manifesting their interest in the spectrum between Wanda's and Eros's extreme responses.

"Regardless of these types of owners, you will be getting a new one as we will not stay together much longer. Change is the Way of the dog. Even without humans, out in the Wild, we are smart and form packs, working together for survival, but we also fight and strive for power. Life changes and we must change to be alive."

"Once in a pack, especially among the males, these quarrels for dominance will escalate until there can be fights, sometimes to the death. Most often the winner allows the loser to run off into the woods to either slink back and join the pack as a submissive member or wander away and be part of the pack no more." Skylark was gaining some momentum with her presentation, having left her emotional baggage behind. "The Way of the dog is that we will not stay together. As your mother, this happens all too soon."

Skylark took a breather, looking over her minions and finding that they were alert, attending to her every thought.

"There are two sides to the Way of the dog—survival and seeking happiness." Skylark's tone of thought changed. "I've harped on surviving, and knowing your owner is potentially a key in understanding how to survive, but happiness is an equal, if not greater part, of the Way of the dog."

"I'm happy!" Wanda quipped sarcastically.

"You need to understand happiness, puppies," she continued. "Some say happiness is pleasure. Others say it is virtue. But it is neither. At the core of happiness is joy. You cannot be happy if you are not joyful about something. When you find this joy, happiness, grace, and virtue will follow. *The Way of the dog* is to find this joy every day and to never give up this search.

"But the Way of the dog is a conundrum too. Emotions can be contrary to survival, and during difficult times we seek a calmness, an oasis where emotions do not exist. However, we aspire to achieve happiness, which is an emotion. In essence, we do not want emotions, but so too, we do want emotions."

"Are we supposed to remember this?" Matt asked. Since he had a near eidetic memory, Matt did not really have a memory issue. The lack of desire to understand what he remembered was his issue.

"Maybe this is a lot to learn." His mother slowed down. "I am covering too much for you to take in, I know, but it is better to introduce you to the Way of the dog. If necessary, I can go over aspects of the Way that you don't understand at another time."

Skylark noticed Eros was perpetually and perceptibly fidgeting.

"Okay, Eros," his mother said and smiled. "Questions?"

"I am confused," Eros said, admitting to himself that confusion was a natural state for him. He was always confused, and from his confusion arose his questions. "If happiness is joy, isn't joy in happiness?"

"Joy comes in short bursts of energy," Mother said and nodded affirmatively as if to say, "Good question." "And happiness is the residue after joy passes."

Eros cocked his head to his right side, obviously not grasping Skylark's assertion.

"My joy blossomed when you were born," Skylark clarified. "My happiness extended that joy into my daily life, supported by the pleasures you bestow on me as I bring you up and teach you the challenges of being a dog, but this feeling of happiness is as ephemeral as our last few weeks. Joy is eternal."

"Joy?"

"Joy is somewhat inexpressible, but it is like the joy I felt when I first mingled my thoughts with all of you and taught you how to use mingling. Joy rejuvenates my happiness. When I greeted you in life and we mingled for the first time, I felt great joy, a blast of lightning striking my soul, but like an early morning mist, the memory of that joy burns off with the heat of the day and in the face of the facts of the reality of daily life."

"Mingle?" Matt asked. Being overly encumbered with the practicalities of surviving, he had not troubled himself worrying about intellectual details, so he had not bothered to learn much about how the puppies and his mother communicated. He just did it and did not concern himself about how he did it. Mingling was still a foreign concept to him. Matt was never concerned about learning the process, and Skylark did not push it.

"If you don't think about something, you can't ask about it and forget about understanding it!" Eros commented to himself, but he held back voicing his comment.

"Yes, our telepathy is sort of a mingling of our minds. Not only do we communicate, but I also share some of my experiences." Since Matt asked the least number of questions, Skylark smiled and elaborated, while the rest of her puppies painfully squirmed, not wanting to go over this *old stuff.* "How do you know anything when you have never experienced it before? How do you know and telepathically speak words you have never heard before? I have shared my knowledge with you. That is how!"

"Is there a perfect procedure to find this joy?" Eros interrupted, trying to divert the conversation into something he thought would be more interesting—in other words, new stuff, not old stuff. He was bored by Matt's diversion into the subject of mingling, a subject that Eros thought he knew fully. (Silly dog! Your knowledge can never be complete.)

"No, there are many practices, but none are perfect. All the procedures have one commonality. You can only find joy if you put aside all distractions. Anger, desires, and expectations must all be removed from your mind, and then joy can find you." Mother nodded knowingly. "To find joy, you must be found."

"What's procedure?" Eros did not realize that he had brought this word up himself.

"A perfect example of advanced mingling!" Skylark said, jerking the conversation back to Matt's line of questioning. "In regard to mingling, the process is not perfect. Nothing is perfect for that matter. For instance, where did you come up with the word *procedure*, Eros?"

"Uh…" His mother's change of pace surprised Eros.

"This word has never been spoken between us, but here you have it," Skylark forged on while Eros mentally stammered. "While we've telepathically touched and talked, the rest of our minds mingled, and you received additional knowledge unknowingly. You obtained a word without understanding what it means."

Deferring but also concurring, Eros received some more thoughts and understood that procedure was a process of staring at Mary with a request in mind and waiting for Mary to respond, which she would inevitably do. His mother's example related to making Mary put food down. Skylark would sit in paradise and stare at Mary until Mary got enough telepathic thoughts to seep through her thick layer of thoughts to realize that Skylark (Shyla) was hungry and needed to be fed. Eros recognized this ritual as his mother's *procedure* for getting food on a regular basis from Mary, but she would use this same process—stare, think, penetrate Mary's thoughts—to be let out into the Wild or into the kennel to be with her pups.

"Does that help, Matt?" Skylark asked, disconnecting from Eros's telepathic sidetrack. "You understand mingling better?"

Matt mumbled a response, saying that he had had enough; whether he understood or not was another matter.

"What do humans seek?" Wanda stirred.

"There are so many humans with many paths, but very few seek joy or even know they should be seeking joy. A preponderance of these people think you have to seek virtue before joy can find you. This is the thinking that the tail goes before the nose."

"Virtue?" Charley perked up at this topic, which attribute would be expected of an emulator of the gallant green dog.

"Dogs find joy whenever and wherever they can, and after being touched, they are blessed often with happiness." Mother continued. "Grace and virtue follow in due course in that order."

"I don't understand how joy, happiness, grace, and virtue go together," Wanda spoke up. Eros was glad that he was not the only pup asking questions.

"Dogs don't search for grace or virtue. They seek joy, and dogs see joy everywhere—that is, if life allows them to live to enjoy it. Joy teaches us happiness, and happiness teaches us grace; this grace when viewed by others is described as virtue. There are many paths that could be called virtuous, but all start with joy. When you lose the distraction of your self-interest, you will enter a state of grace, which leads to a life, which is perceived as being virtuous."

"So joy manifests like a flower!" Artemis offered a simile. "As the flower wilts, the petals that are scattered about are shards of happiness, and whoever humbly gathers those petals and wishes to give those petals away are living in a state of grace. Without material desires, grace emanates throughout your life, and naturally, virtue can be seen in your footsteps like footprints in the snow."

"Snow?" Eros asked. He was duly ignored.

"Dogs are not arrogant enough to pretend that they can be made virtuous through an act of will. This is false virtue and does not assure access to the path of happiness. Because of this awareness— the nose going before the tail, we feel that we receive joy more frequently than other creatures." Skylark continued Artemis's line of thought. "We live with life, but dogs are not foolish to think we can dictate life. This innate humility and the knowledge that we seek joy are what separate dogs from the rest of the beasts on the earth."

Eros realized from mingling that *beasts* included humans plus an assortment of other creatures he was not yet acquainted with.

"When will our puppy family be split apart?" As was his way, Eros's mind leaped jaggedly into this unexpected issue, circling back to the beginning of the conversation. Skylark noted that he sliced through the conversation like Occam's razor through a philosophical knot of ideas.

"Good question to end our discussion on." Skylark's compliment left the grumpy Eros feeling better. "That is part of the Way! In truth, our family could have been torn apart at any time before now. The call of the Wild tears your life apart and puts it back together according to its own whims. Since I have conveyed to you the Way of the dog, I am at peace. When the time comes, you are ready to move on!"

Skylark's children were graduating from puppy kindergarten and would be soon going on to the rest of their lives. These happy and sad feelings merged within her as she looked over her brood with melancholy eyes. (Stuck-up stoics would not approve such a manifestation of emotion!)

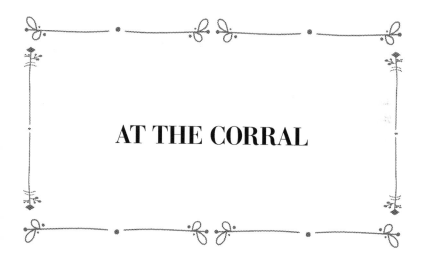

# AT THE CORRAL

"**D**on't go to the barn!" Skylark declared vehemently, fixing her worst evil eye on her children. Beware a mother's anger! It is fiercer than the fiercest storm! That was the impression Skylark had left in the minds of her puppies.

About a week after the little pack's first foray into the Wild, the pups were let loose again. No longer enamored with the sky, the clouds, the dirt, and the grass, the pups spread out wide across the yard. When Mother went off after Matt and Wanda as they wandered too far into the pasture in her estimation, she was not looking in Eros's direction. Unsurprisingly, he took advantage of this lack of oversight and went straight toward the barn, running hard. Eros wanted the most time he could get to snoop around.

Artemis followed along, fussing, "Mama said not to go to the barn."

Artemis probably said this several more times, but Eros was not listening. In what felt like an instant, he was at the corral next to the barn with Artemis following up, remonstrating with him.

"We need to go back," she cried. "Mama's going to be angry!"

"And whoooo are you?" A deep bass voice echoed in their thoughts followed by a heavy snort. Artemis was shocked into silence. Abruptly, she turned and hightailed it back to the house. Artemis's abrupt departure couldn't sway Eros from asking his questions.

"You're a horse, aren't you?" Eros didn't hesitate to ask this question. He was relentless. "What do you do? Are you going to stomp on me?"

"Well, little fella," the deep voice went on, interrupting the pup. "If I can see you, I won't stomp you, but you've got to keep out from under my hooves."

"Hooves? Oh, yes, hooves!" Eros had never seen hooves and went directly under the horse to inspect them.

"Watch out down there! I can't move until you're where I can see you." The deep voice drawled. Taking a deep breath, he snorted loudly. "Are you done?"

"What kind of horse are you? A palomino? An Arabian?" Emerging from underneath the horse to the horse's great relief, Eros could not stop himself from rattling off these questions. He was so excited. "A mustang? An Andalusian or a Clydesdale?"

"I'm mostly a Morgan, although there are rumors I have a touch of American Cream in my ancestry," the stately brown-haired beast responded, putting his head over the corral and fixing his amber eyes on Eros. "I have never heard so many questions come from a dog before. You must be Eros, the metaphysical dog!"

Eros stopped short, reining in all his questions, all except one.

"How did you know that I'm Eros?"

"I talk to Skylark." The horse shook his whole head up and down, nodding. "She is a nice dog, and she is very proud of her pups."

"But she told us to avoid the barn." Eros suspected a double-standard.

"You're young and stupid," the horse rationalized. "She probably thought you wouldn't know better and would run under my hooves when I wasn't looking, or you might bother the pigs or sheep, and they might get after you. In either case, you could be hurt."

"Because Mary rides you and whips you to a mindless frenzy, you stomp on poor wee creatures?" Eros's questions were gearing back up again. "Or is it because you just can't look down to see what's under your hooves?"

"Rather! She never whips me!" the horse said, stiffening visibly at this undignified suggestion. "I can see my feet too! Problem is, I can't see under all my hooves all the time."

"I'm sorry if I upset you," Eros assured him.

"No matter," the horse said, softening his stance. "As to the other stuff, where do you get all these questions? Skylark says you question everything! How do you know so much about horses?"

"Questions just explode in my brain. I don't know where they come from," Eros replied. "About horses, Mary thinks about them all the time and talks about riding you. That's why I know about so many types of horses! She dreams of buying a palomino, but then she decides it would cost too much and thinks about another breed and decides she wants to get one of them. Again, this new horse costs too much. Unfortunately, she can't afford any purebred horse. Nevertheless, she likes thinking about them."

"Ah," the horse understood. "So that is how you know all about horses?"

"Yes, I guess I am an expert." Eros was puffing up with pride, not realizing that he was far from an expert at anything.

"Do you know about me?" The horse was shaking his head back and forth, whinnying gently. "Do you even know my name?"

Like a little puffer fish puffed to its maximum, Eros had gone from fat and ready to explode to deflated, all the puff of his arrogant pride whistling out of him.

"No," the humbled little puppy admitted.

"Buck up, little pup. You'll learn that my owners had delusions of grandeur for me and called me Hercules."

"You're Hercules?"

"Yes, like the Greek hero," the horse said, neighing jovially "I am just a horse. No cleaning stables for me. I just fill them up!"

Eros received fitful minglings from Hercules, as if they were incomplete sentences, but one mingle that he got loud and clear was the image of Hercules relieving himself in a stall inside the barn.

"You're allowed to go in the barn?" Eros was aghast.

"Not only allowed, I am encouraged," Hercules proudly declared. "Makes it easier for Mary to pick up and reuse somewhere else on the farm."

Recently, having started a regimen of house training, Eros was irate that a horse could go inside while he was being forced to go outside. This seemed fundamentally unfair to him, but calmed down when he realized and rationalized, *Fairness is not among life's priorities.*

"I have never seen you plowing the field," Eros snapped, showing a bit of his anger. He was following up on one of Mary's fantasies in which Hercules plowed the field and pulled a fancy buggy through the streets downtown.

"Never have, never will!" Hercules agreed. "I'm around for Mary to ride. This isn't a fully working farm. There's just me, four pigs, a bunch of sheep, and a horde of chickens."

"Pigs?" Not only was Eros interested in this particular farm animal on an intellectual level, he couldn't resist saying the word *pig* since he found it amusing. Using this word also allowed his anger to decompress.

"Yep, they are very clever creatures, them there pigs, but it is like they're having a soap opera in the barn. Or should I say a drama in their dreams? Most of 'em have highfalutin ideas of what they are!"

Eros listened attentively, looking up at the horse who towered above him. The little dog sat on his haunches with his front legs straight, head tilted up. Eros was perplexed by Hercules's last comment, but he only showed this by cocking his head to the right.

"There's an old saying about a tempest in a teapot," Hercules said and nodded his head, chuckling at the humor found in life. "Well, this barn is a teapot, and those four pigs have as many stormy intrigues as can fill a world."

"The world is huge," Eros marveled, wondering how pigs could fill it up.

"The world is as big as your imagination," Hercules said. "The pigs can't see beyond the front doors of the barn, and to tell you the truth, they don't see the doors no more either. They have no imagination! Without imagination, you don't look beyond your feed trough."

"But the doors are so big." Eros marveled at the proclivity of creatures to see and not see what they wanted to. "How can they not see the doors?"

"Pigs are pigs, but they don't look up much neither," Hercules rattled on. "But they do talk to themselves. The way they argue among themselves, it feels as if there were one hundred pigs in there, not just four."

Eros was a little mystified by this last comment.

"You'll see. There's Zeus and Aphrodite, Prometheus and Athena," Hercules recounted from memory. "Mary likes them Greek god and goddess names, but she is starting to run out of them when it comes to the pups. As I understand, Artemis and you are the only ones named after a Greek goddess or god in this litter."

"Me?"

"Didn't know that, did you?" Hercules was proud of his superior knowledge. As all creatures become aware that they know more than someone else, anyone else, at some point, there can be a moment when the weak glorify themselves in their superiority. Hercules immersed himself in such a moment, backing off the fence, strutting about the corral, tail up and flourishing. Once the moment passed, Hercules jauntily came back to talk with Eros.

"Was that necessary?" Eros inquired.

"I'm just showing you how us horses are superior to all other creatures."

"I respectfully disagree," Eros piped up. "My mother says dogs are the ultimate creature on earth followed by humans, horses, and then the rest of living creatures."

Eros fudged, adding horses just behind humans and excluding the reference to inferior creatures. He didn't want to hurt the horse's feelings, and he didn't want to sound pompous by using the word *inferior.*"

"That's just hooey!" Hercules announced with a large whinny-laugh. "Of course your mother would say that. No offense to Skylark, but the facts are the facts. Am I bigger than you? Yes! Am I smarter than you? Yes!" (He was referring to his knowledge about Eros's name as the proof for this statement.) "Am I faster than you? Of course! Does Skylark love me more than you? Yes!"

"Yip," Eros objected. "Skylark loves me more!"

"I'm sure she does, sort of! Your mother goes through litter after litter, but who is still here after all the pups have come and gone?" Hercules looked as if he was tying his argument up in a big blue ribbon. "Hercules is always here. That's my criterion!"

Hercules logic was flawless, or so Eros thought. He didn't know what to say. To begin with, Eros didn't know what a criterion was. He could communicate with Hercules, but mingling with horses was somewhat patchy since he did not get as much consistent background information as with Skylark.

"Does the longer one loves mean the more one loves?" Eros attempted to ask a number of questions, reconnoitering Hercules's logic.

"Yes, that's it." Hercules heard Eros's thought and interrupted his cogitations. Hercules confirmed that Eros had just outlined his theory of love. "By that logic, Skylark loves me more than you!"

"Or a love with more intensity for a shorter period of time represent 'more love'? That would mean my mother would love me more than you!" Eros struggled since this was metaphysics way above his current knowledge, but this rationale seemed reasonable.

"That's the Romeo and Juliet theory," Hercules snorted. "A lot of hooey for human teenagers!"

"I don't know which is right, Hercules. I'm not even a teenager yet."

Hercules thought about it and decided it was not worth arguing this point until Eros was a bit bigger.

"No matter...for now! Before I forget, there are five sheep, Makai, Marty, Melissa, Myrtle, and Mirabelle. They're none too bright, but they think they are. For some reason, Mary named 'em differently, no Greek gods there. Said something about them being fodder for the Sirens?"

"I think that is about something mindlessly following something," Eros recalled Mary thinking about the Sirens.

"Skylark's list should put the chickens in a different category since they are so dumbstruck all the time." Hercules nodded to the side of the yard behind his back, where half a dozen chickens were pecking about his paddock.

"Mama didn't list by intelligence. At least I don't think she did," Eros responded. Over the course of their conversation, he gathered that the word *criterion* meant some method of measuring. Curious, Eros wondered what criterion Skylark had used when he was rudely jarred awake from his musings.

"Oh, by the way, talking about Skylark, guess who's coming this way?"

"Huh, Mother?"

"Sure looks like she wants a piece of your hide to mount on her doghouse wall. Think I'll just mosey over here for a while." Hercules was smart enough to know when to get out of the line of fire, and it didn't take much figuring to prophesize that fire was going to rain down on poor Eros *tout suite*.

Without too much ado, Skylark did what Skylark does, be a mother...

# THE STORY OF MAZZIE

About three days after Eros's visit to the corral, the pups played all day. They were so revved up that they could not settle down no matter how many times their mother told them to take it easy.

"Okay, pups," Skylark announced. "You can't calm down, so I am going to tell you a scary story."

"I've heard of those! Is it a horror story?" Wanda yipped, expressing her enthusiasm. Youngsters want to hear about the most gruesome things, and Wanda was a youngster, for sure.

"Yes, there are some very horrible parts," Mother said, "but it has a happy ending."

"How can scary have a happy ending?" Eros asked incredulously. "How scary is scary?"

"Why don't you tell me?" His mother cut him short, showing a bit of annoyance with his incessant questioning.

"Tell us! Tell us!" the other pups shouted, eager to hear a story.

"Okay. Snuggle down!" Skylark ordered. Once the pups had found comfortable positions, she started.

*"Mazzie was born on a dark and stormy night, a gloomy harbinger of the future she was to endure. A female, she was what humans call a mutt, not purebred like you, my little miniature pumpkins, but a nice dog nonetheless."*

"What's a pumpkin?" Eros asked.

"A bulbous orange fruit!" Artemis obliged. From that description, Eros had a big pumpkin pop into his brain.

"I'm not orange," Eros objected to the brightness of the color.

"Okay, you are more a yellowish gold," Skylark admitted, and a pumpkin with a softer golden color arose in his thoughts, more in keeping with his coat.

"Why are you saying I am like plants? I'm not bulbous and lumpy. I'm lean and long and—"

"Eros, that's enough!" Skylark raised her eyes in exasperation. "Let me get back to the story!"

Eros grumbled his way to silence, and at the end of the rumble of his last grumble, Skylark resumed.

*Mazzie was born on a dark and stormy night, a gloomy harbinger of the future she was to endure. A mutt, she was somewhere between a golden retriever and a Labrador. Mazzie had a beautiful brown coat, and she could run faster than a rabbit. When she stood at attention,*

smelling the air, Mazzie was a regal sight—that is, if one overlooked her pedigree.

Mazzie had a decent puppyhood since she was brought up with her siblings, and she had a good mother. (All dog mothers are good mothers, if life allows.) Her breeder was unremarkable, neither good nor bad, but the dark days of her life began on another dark and gloomy day, pivoting on a dark decision by her breeder.

"How much?" an unhappy dark-haired man asked.

"She's gotten too old, nine months, you can have her for cheap. Just pay for her shots," Mazzie's breeder, a fat, dumpy man, stated.

"Too much!"

In the background were rows and rows of cages, dogs barking right and left, expressing various shades of their dissatisfaction. "I'm hungry!" "I'm thirsty!" "Let me out!"

"How much you got?" The fat, dumpy man was hoping to offset some of his costs. The tubby owner kept his kennels in good order, but dogs were not real to him, just pieces of meat to buy and sell. When the occasion arose, this attitude converted this marginally respectable owner into a bad owner.

"I'll give you five bucks, but she has to have all her shots, and I want her neutered too."

"Five dollars!"

"Forget about it!"

"Wait! Okay, okay…" The fat dumpy man wasn't totally bad, but he was far from good. The owner did keep the puppies healthy out of self-interest, yet he had no interest in the feelings of his charges. Unfortunately, self-interest can lead anyone astray, as this owner teetered between bad and sleazy.

The offer was brutal. Nevertheless, the dumpy man reasoned that it was time to cut his losses with this bitch.

"Isn't *bitch* a bad word?" Artemis asked.

"That is what we are, my dear. You and me," Artemis's mother responded.

Eros was irked by the thought, *Why can Mother ignore my questions and not Artemis's?*

"All female dogs are bitches, and all bitches are beautiful! Humans have such twisted views of reality, and this is one of them. They take a beautiful word and make it bad, but you must forgive their inaneness. Humans are good. Unfortunately, they don't know when they are, but let me continue."

*The deal between breeder and customer was done, and this new owner—his name was Clark—took Mazzie with him, calling her Dummy. Right off the bat, Mazzie knew she was in trouble.*

*Over the next six months, Clark beat her every night for any insignificant reason he could think of or sometimes just because he felt like it. One day Clark was shooting off his shotgun and thought he came up with something funny. Clark kicked Mazzie into the center of a field and yelled, "Hey, Dummy! Go! Run!"*

*Mazzie was dazed, and although she knew the command, she was so distraught that she couldn't move. Frustrated, Clark walked about thirty feet away, turned, and shot both barrels of his shotgun in Mazzie's direction. Mazzie felt something hit her rump like a bee sting, and she was off.*

*"This is a blast!" Clark exclaimed, laughing while reloading his gun. He thought this was hilarious, guffawing loudest when a pellet hit Mazzie again, and she jumped at the injury. "Run, Dummy! Run!"*

*"Forgive humans, for they know not what they do!" Mazzie recalled what she had learned from her mother.*

"That's from The Book of the Dog!" Charley excitedly blurted.

"Yes, her mother had taught Mazzie well, but what does this mean?" Skylark asked. She moved on quickly before anyone attempted to answer her rhetorical question, especially Eros, who would probably jump in with a bunch of questions. "If you catch a mouse in the house and it bites you before you kill it, do you stay mad at it? No, you forgive the poor creature and forget it bit you before you eat it. The mouse didn't know it shouldn't have bitten you. The same goes for humans. This awareness is at the heart of humility, and most humans haven't any idea on how to be humble. They just don't know that they are fools being foolish."

After looking around, their mother resumed.

*After numerous explosions, Clark stopped shooting. (Mazzie didn't know how many times the shotgun went off exactly. She wasn't that good at counting, especially not when adrenaline was pumping through her veins.) He was laughing his head off, as he finally indicated that they were leaving. "C'mon, Dummy! I'm outta shotgun shells…"*

*For all the bluster and blasting, Mazzie ended up with just five pellets and some mild bleeding. Clark did nothing to fix her up. To his credit, Clark never leveled the shotgun directly at Mazzie, or she wouldn't have survived; however, this is just extolling a particular tint across various shades of stupidity.*

*These were dark days that moved into months and then years, but Mazzie found ways to survive. Her memories of puppyhood sustained her hope that someday she may find happiness.*

"Remember, pups, the Way of the dog is to survive!" Skylark stopped for a moment to look at each pup.

"Could it have been Mazzie's fault?" Matt took the low road in analyzing the story.

"No, Matt, I can think of two reasons why this didn't work," Skylark answered. "After Mazzie had been with Clark for two years, the man decided he didn't like Mazzie anymore, but one could reasonably question whether Clark liked Mazzie to begin with."

"And the second?" Artemis followed closely.

"An alternative hypothesis is that owners want dogs to be a reflection of themselves and that Clark got Mazzie to punish himself, as he felt he was being punished by life. Either way, Clark is the villain of this story because he clung to his ignorance, and this neglect stimulated his anger. This cycle of ignorance and anger viciously twirled in his mind so much that he couldn't realize who he was or what he wanted."

"Do dogs always apologize for the imperfections of their owners?" Eros slipped in a question.

"We have to." His mother deigned to answer one of his questions. "All humans are imperfect, but they avoid this awareness of themselves. In regard to Clark, he has no excuse for being an idiot."

"If dogs are more perfect than humans, why are dogs' life spans so short?" Eros insisted on inserting another question.

"Because God allows dogs to get more perfect every day," Mother explained. "Once a dog achieves pure perfection, it is his or her time to become one with the One again. Humans never reach perfection. Even the most perfect of humans are imperfect. In the end, dogs go to heaven, whereas humans just die."

Skylark swept everyone's attention back to the story without hesitation, not allowing Eros to slip in another question, as she continued.

*Recognizing at least that he no longer wanted Mazzie around, Clark decided one stormy morning (all bad days seem to be stormy days in stories) to take Mazzie out in the countryside and kick her out of the car into the drizzling rain after removing her collar with her dog tags.*

*She was abandoned in the Wild. This was the worst! The first twenty-four hours she just sat in the rain, licking her face for water.*

*For five days she lived in the Wild. At night it felt like horrors were just around the corner. Because of these fears, she couldn't sleep at night, and during the day she wandered around to find a nearby stream to drink from. But food was either scant or nonexistent. The worst of the worst was when Mazzie wished to be back with Clark. She was on the edge of giving up hope.*

*At the beginning Mazzie waited near the place where Clark had left her. As crazy as it sounds, she was expecting Clark to return to pick her up, but to no avail. As delusional as this may be, Mazzie still believed that underneath it all, Clark loved her as she loved him.*

*Soon, Mazzie's fears became greater than the challenges she faced. The horrors of the Wild overwhelmed her thoughts. Owls swooped down at her, but she ducked before they could take her head off. She hid from the dog-eating deer as well. Fear from all the boogey-dog stories wore her down, making her cringe at every cracking twig. (Human boogeyman stories are nothing compared to dogdom's versions.)*

*Mazzie withstood these terrors for days, but after the rain stopped, hunger eventually drove her to wander farther into the Wild and away from where Clark had left her. To a minor degree, this change in strategy was successful, yielding an occasional field mouse that she wolfed down.*

*Pushing through thickets and wild hedges, she wandered aimlessly. Everything was Wild. The hedges felt like they flayed the flesh from her bones while Mazzie squeezed through. After passing through this gauntlet, there were many prickles painfully embedded in her skin under her fur.*

*And meat-eating deer chased her across the field of corn. (The deer never moved—they just stared, but in Mazzie's mind the deer's eyes pursued her like big balloons until she was out of their sight.)*

*Mazzie was desperately lost, and she had no place to go—that is, until she came across a cottage next to the disheveled cornfield that she had just navigated.*

Skylark paused for breath.

"Deer are dog-eaters?" Eros asked, taking advantage of the moment.

"Dog-eaters and man-eaters!" His mother quickly confirmed this fact, but hurried back to her story so Eros could not ask another question.

*Oh...* Eros took this in, amazed at his mother's worldly knowledge as Skylark continued.

*In Mazzie's imagination, the cornfield was sprinkled with other unseen dangers, snakes popping out of holes, and scarecrows with jack-o'-lantern heads flying after her. Gathering her courage, she negotiated these terrors, figuring it was easier to fight off a real attack than worry about a hundred attacks waiting to happen. Exhausted by days of suffering in the harsh Wild, she made it up to the small house.*

*Mazzie arrived during the night, and all she could do was sit near the front door, whimpering. She thought she had whimpered for hours on end, but in reality, after fifteen minutes, the door flung open. There was a light of glory blazing behind a silhouette (at least the glory was what Mazzie thought she saw). The figure took the form of a lithe young woman who shouted, "Who's there?"*

*Mazzie heard the words blasting over and in her like God speaking from the mountain, but maybe the woman did not really shout. Maybe Mazzie was so paralyzed with fear that any sound was amplified. Nevertheless, she could not move, and she curled into a fetal position. Unbeknownst to Mazzie, she was still whimpering quietly, even though the whimpers were muffled.*

*"Oh-ho!" The woman exclaimed, spotting the dog at the edge of the light. Mazzie cringed when the human discovered her, but she was too scared and famished to run off.*

*"What's up, girl?" With that, the woman came over to Mazzie, who was just outside the arc of the outdoor light. Slowly, the woman*

approached Mazzie with gentleness and respect, and Mazzie began feeling she may survive.

The new human's name was Crystal, and after a while of gentle petting and soft, soothing talk, the woman asked Mazzie if she wanted to go in the cabin with her. Then when Crystal realized Mazzie wasn't able to move, paralyzed with fear, she picked up the emaciated forty-pound dog and carried Mazzie into her home.

Crystal nursed Mazzie back to health, taking all the prickles off her patient and washing her up. During the bathing process, Crystal found bumps under Mazzie's skin. When Mazzie was healthy enough, Crystal took Mazzie to the veterinarian, who told Crystal that the bumps were from buckshot. He subsequently removed the shrapnel while Mazzie was under anesthesia at Crystal's insistence.

Mazzie had developed enough of a rapport with Crystal that she put aside the fear she associated with Clark abandoning her and placed all her trust in this woman. Before she went to the vet, Crystal was asked the dog's name when she made the appointment. Crystal approached the cringing dog, and they communed for a while, eye to eye, almost head to head, during which time Crystal was murmuring, "What should I call you?"

"I've got it. I'll call you Macy!" Crystal had an epiphany.

Mazzie was ecstatic. She knew an owner coming up with a name so close to her real one was a very good omen, and this development supported the trust that Mazzie put in Crystal. The story ends with Mazzie living happily ever after with Crystal in the cottage by the golden cornfield. The end! Skylark finally said with emphasis.

Solemnly, his mother concluded her harrowing tale, but Eros later speculated that it could actually be her own story (though he never confirmed his suspicion).

"This fable is about the Way of the dog! If you survive, you can find happiness, and if survival is a struggle, you never give up!" Skylark stated.

When Skylark actually looked at her pups, they were all fast asleep, all except one, Eros.

"Eros, no questions," his mother chided him. "Go to sleep!"

And to her surprise, he did.

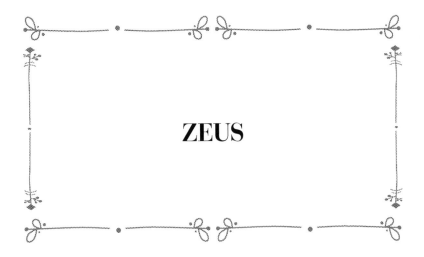

# ZEUS

After four days, Skylark finally stopped berating Eros for going to the barn. Eros had explained that he only went to the corral, not the barn, but his mother just saw that argument as splitting hairs. Eros had been a bad, bad puppy!

At the time of discovery, she had crossed the yard in seconds and bounced Eros around like a pinball all the way back to the house, but this wasn't the bad part. The psychological scolding lasted much longer. Humans think they have it bad. Once the shouting stops, a human can lay low. When dealing with telepathy, Eros's scolding echoed through his thoughts for a full twenty-four hours, cutting him over and over. He could not hide and lick his mental wounds until this reverberating reprimand subsided.

Eros curbed his curiosity as much as he could, appeasing Skylark, but it was a struggle not going to the barn because he had so many questions. At the end of this week of hell, Eros felt he had as many questions waiting to burst forth as he had hairs on his body. Since he was a furry little body that was a lot of questions, and a lot of extended hair follicles. Eros imagined himself as a poodle sticking his paw into a light socket with all the fur on his body sticking straight out.

Ready to explode, when Skylark settled down for a nap one afternoon, Eros seized the opportunity and took off at a full gallop for the red barn. Hercules's head swung quickly from left to right as Eros raced past his corral, aiming for the large barn doors, which had been left partially open.

The barn had two large front doors, and above those, there were a set of two smaller doors providing access to an upper level that was for storing hay for the winter. Hanging on rollers at the top, these two big doors weren't easy to move around. Hence, it was a rarity when the doors were completely shut. Fortunately, there was always enough wiggle room for a puppy to squeeze through.

Under the roof of the barn, Eros found it was darker than outside yet somewhat luminous too, as if the light seeped in from all angles. The atmosphere was pungent. For a human, the barn was a place of darker corners and obnoxious odors, but for a dog this was a magical place where the fascinating odors interlaced with the light permeating the air, producing, a church-like glow and feel to the interior.

The barn itself was relatively small, and the interior layout was like an upside-down U split by a large central section. After entering through the front hanging doors, there was a small open alcove to the right and left. Nothing was on the right side, but on the wall was a ladder to the upper level. In the left nook, there was a table and a wooden chair. Papers presumably related to the farm business were stacked on the left side of the table, while a small desk lamp with a green shade was on the right.

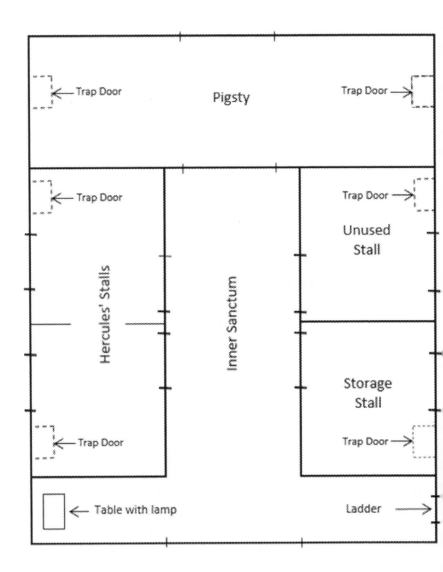

Trap Door

Pigsty

Trap Door

Trap Door

Trap Door

Unused Stall

Hercules' Stalls

Inner Sanctum

Storage Stall

Trap Door

Trap Door

Table with lamp

Ladder

Beyond these small areas, there were two stalls on each side, right and left, with split doors to the interior corridor, which were half open, and full doors leading to the outside. Next to each exterior stall door was a window. At the far end of the barn, a wide area was blocked off, which could have been two stalls, and originally an interior section, joined and lined up across the back of the barn, but this section had been reconfigured in such a way as to make one large horizontal stall, which contained the pigsty.

There were two doors to the right and left exterior walls, but these were sealed with putty and were inaccessible behind water and feed troughs. Each of these doors had a window next to them.

There was an upper level for the storage of hay, but that was only accessible via the ladder and the upper-level front door. Smaller drop-down trap doors existed above every stall over the cubicle's window so that the farmer could throw down hay into each stall when needed. The large horizontal stall had trap doors over its two windows on the right and left sides.

The first stall on the left was the only stall with the exterior door open. Hercules clumped in from the paddock through this door, curious about how Eros would fare with the pigs. Hercules was pampered, living in both of the stalls on the left. The interior wall between the two stalls had been removed to make one long vertically shaped stall.

On the right were two empty stalls, side by side. The first, the one nearest the front door, had a stash of hay bales stacked up, indicating that the hay for the winter had already been stored in the hayloft with the excess overflowing into this stall. Nearest the pigsty, the second stall on the right was empty, but it was nicely laid out with clean hay covering the floor. It looked like an animal could move in at a moment's notice.

At the back of the small barn, the horizontal stall created a makeshift pigsty with a fence with a latched gate patched together with two-by-fours and wire mesh fencing. Exactly opposite the front hanging doors, the pigs could look into the middle of the barn but not slip through the slats of the fence or gate.

At the far end of the barn off the pigsty, there were exterior doors matching the front doors, and these were permanently open. There was also a two-by-four fence and gate fitted inside the frame of this door, which incidentally afforded the pigs at this door a panoramic view of the pastures behind the barn.

Both these wire mesh arrangements, the fence and the gate, helped facilitate ventilation as the odor would otherwise be staggering. There was a small awning above the outside door so the pigsty near the outside door would be well shaded.

Fascinated, Eros approached the pigs quietly.

"How dare you approach your god?" The nearest pig boomed. "How have you the nerve to speak to the Almighty Me in my Inner Sanctum?"

"I, sir, I—" Eros meekly stammered. "I haven't spoken."

"Meek! I like meek! I am impressed, so you may continue..." While this large pig deigned to let Eros enter his presence, Eros noted the pig's inconsistent comments, which inconsistency he learned was a particular trait of this pig. "You have not been like other dogs who have come here and barked viciously and asked to enter our presence very rudely. What is thine name, courteous dog?"

"Eros, sir." Eros was on the verge of turning around and bolting back out the door. "I was not aware that gods existed on the farm."

"Come forth, Eros!" the pig boomed. Eros was expecting lightning and gale force winds to come down on him, but only the pig's breath, which was not very pleasant, even for a dog, passed across Eros's face. "I am Zeus, although some call me Deus. I am known as the god of all gods!"

Eros dawdled, not doing anything since he was a bit confused. His mother said that dogs were the superior species, whereas Hercules said horses were. Now a pig blasted both those cosmologies apart by being a god.

"Sire, king of the gods," Eros hesitantly said. "Hercules was telling me that horses were the greatest species. I don't understand where pigs fit, your most holy swine?"

"I like that greeting! I am the holiest swine of all swine!" Zeus was enamored with the virtues of this salutation. Catching himself, he continued, "Naturally, the horse would think otherwise. All he thinks of is himself and his so-called advantages—how fast he can run, how high he can jump, even how big his farts are."

Zeus stopped to take a breath. It appeared that gods breathed, or at least this one did.

"Contrary to what he says, I have much superior farts than his, but I digress. These are frivolous concerns!" This time Zeus stopped for effect, not for breath. "Gods are above these petty fears. Since pigs are the height of evolution, we must be gods. There are gods, animals, and vermin."

"Can't vermin be animals?"

"*Don't argue with me, pup*! *You* don't ask questions of your *god*, especially questions your god doesn't want to answer!" Zeus boomed, deciding to answer in spite of his own wrath. "Rats and humans are vermin right alongside horseflies and other insects. I consider them beneath animals."

"Oh..." Eros was taken aback by Zeus's instantly aggressive attitude and very negative analysis of humans. Eros liked Mary, and he couldn't conceive of her as being equivalent to an insect. Eros also noted to himself that Zeus's categorization was primitive and inconsistent.

"Humans and insects are different types of creatures. Vermin can't be both animals and insects. It doesn't make sense," Eros blurted out.

"*You don't argue with a god*," Zeus yelled at Eros and then turned his head, offering his profile. "I am the god of gods, and I can do anything I please. Whatever I do makes sense regardless of how nonsensical it is."

"Er..." Eros was again taken aback by the forcefulness of the pig's last response, not to mention the circularity of Zeus's logic. Seeking a less controversial tack, Eros decided to follow a different line of questioning. "What other gods are there?"

"Aphrodite, Prometheus, and Athena are here, and there are many more besides them. Apollo was here, but he went on ahead. He is acting as my emissary to Mount Olympus, preparing the way for my ascension."

"You mean he went to market!" Hercules laughed with a hearty neigh in the background.

"Imbecile, everyone knows gods are immortal!" Zeus ignored the ignorant horse. If you ignore the truth, the truth dissipates, and you are left with the illusion of what you believe, right or wrong. Then you start calling that delusion the truth. "I have been thinking of adding horse to the vermin category."

"Sire, it must be a burden to be the god of gods," Eros stated, asking a question without asking it.

"*It is!* Finally, a creature that understands my sacrifices. All these gods are constantly bickering, and their believers, the pawns of gods, are charged to act out these squabbles with life-and-death battles." Zeus shrugged. "I am the creator, but I am also the peacemaker! I tell them to *shut up!*"

"Must be very effective," Eros concluded, recognizing that Zeus had turned to Aphrodite and Athena, who were arguing loudly about science and religion. Zeus's last two words were shouted, directed at the two females. They did stop arguing–while he was looking at them.

"Very!" Zeus complimented himself, but as he turned his head back to Eros, Aphrodite and Athena resumed their argument in hushed tones. "Yet I need to do it over constantly. It is exhausting being a god! Why do you think I don't talk to humans anymore?"

"Pray, may I talk with the other gods you have assembled here?" Eros attempted to be as gentle with his question as possible.

"I like that! You are praying to me!" Zeus didn't notice that Eros's statement was a question being directed at him, again changing the rules for this conversation on the fly. "Yes, you have my permission to talk with me and the lesser gods!"

The door to the sty was a heavy swinging fence gate with crossbars covered with wire mesh through which Eros and Zeus had spoken. With Zeus's last comment, he moved toward the back of the stall and performed a huge pee. Compressed by the troughs, the stall was tight for the four pigs, and as Zeus moved, the others had to shuffle about in tandem, carrying a different pig to the stall's front door.

Although Eros did not fully apprehend this upon his first visit, the pigsty was a bit small for the four very large pigs in residence. He could not help but notice that the area made for tight quarters, and the thought crossed his mind that, if nothing else, Zeus's head no longer fit regardless of the size.

# APHRODITE

"Hi, and who are you?" Eros attempted to be friendly and open. This was hard to do after dealing with the logically inconsistent and sometimes irascible Zeus.

"I am Aphrodite!" She was very attractive for a pig, Eros thought, and he felt great empathy for her. Aphrodite continued, "I am the goddess of emotion."

"Oh!" Eros was trying to give the impression that he was awestruck. His inherent confusion helped support this impression. From Zeus, he gathered that gods liked this type of adulatory superficiality.

"I suppose you are wondering, *Aren't you the goddess of love?*" Aphrodite urged him on, putting words in Eros's mouth. "History often refers to me as such, not as the goddess of emotion."

"I suppose," the naïve Eros stammered. Eros was not acquainted with much history as of yet, and like the horse, mingling was an important, but imperfect, part of their conversation. Eros noticed that the horse and pigs seemed to have different mingling dialects, which he struggled with to start, but got better at interpreting during his conversations.

"Ah, yes, I knew you would," she responded as if Eros had agreed with her statement. "I am grouped with love and pleasure, but in reality, my domain is all emotions, in which love resides. For example, everyone knows that love and hate are part of the same coin."

"I dunno…. Er…" Eros was taking all this in. Unlike everyone (he assumed), he did not know about love or hate or coins. Aphrodite interpreted his response as him showing her the veneration she deserved. Eros was starting to understand Hercules's comment about the pigs talking to themselves. Although they pretended, the pigs sure weren't talking with him. Eros felt he was a prop for Aphrodite, and whatever he said, she would reinterpret into what she wanted to hear. "Love…ah—"

"You're right! I prefer the nicer emotions, of course," Aphrodite rattled on. "So my affection for love has been misinterpreted, but in the end, I manifest as all emotions. There are so many gradations between love and hate that all emotions get reflected."

"I don't hate," Eros ventured to disagree with her.

"You just don't know yet what you can feel." Aphrodite allowed Eros's comment since the response proved her point. "A perfect example is a man and woman who fall in love and marry, but when they divorce, their capacity for hate is equal to the love they have felt for each other. They have reversed the polarity of their potential emotion, making hate instead of love visible, which leads to their bitter-love parting."

"Let me see if I've got this right," Eros said to the goddess. "A divorce flips your emotions, and the hate you feel is equal to the love you have felt."

"Yes, emotions are so simple, yet everyone wants to make them seem so complex!"

"Hmmm," Eros stated quietly, wondering if emotions could be that simple. Aphrodite was awaiting a deferential display, extolling her awesomeness, but this lackluster, pensive response was all that Eros could muster.

"Yes, I am much more complex and fascinating as the goddess of emotion." Although she was disappointed at the inarticulateness of the puppy, she could not help but be pleased with herself. Eros got the impression that Aphrodite was looking at a mirror, preening herself, even talking to her reflection. He was just a backdrop item on a set at the periphery of her conversation. Although Aphrodite found him disappointing, Eros really had no effect on her conversation with herself.

"Eros? It is Eros?" Aphrodite turned her attention to the little dog, continuing quickly when the puppy didn't instantly respond since she really didn't care what this little beastie's name was. "Emote! You must learn to devote yourself to your emotions. Love, hate, express your love, your anger, your fears! There is nothing but emotions for you to sip from the cup of life. Human's live in the pigsty of emotions!"

"What?" Eros was put back by this last comment as evidenced by his response, but subsequently, he realized that for Aphrodite, the reference to pigsty was for her a compliment.

"I do prefer the emotion of love, but as I try to show humans the wide-ranging wonders of love, they ignore my counsel since they have such a vast propensity to focus on the minuscule, and in particular, the one emotion of hate," Aphrodite said and sighed. "They love to be Rambo'd."

"Rambo'd?" Eros had never heard this term before.

"Yes, I am glad you are aware of this phenomenon," Aphrodite misinterpreted his response as she had done many times before. "Rambo was a fictional human character. I believe he is from the movies, and he loved to hate and loved to consummate his hate by killing what he hated, making him feel that he was righteous and justified to do so. He believed that this consummation of his hate gave him some sort of pleasure!"

"Even humans aren't that bad!" Eros stated, relying on his vast knowledge of humans, thinking of Mary, the only human that he knew.

"You *are* young!" Aphrodite said and chuckled. "Humans are like chickens, sometimes empty-headed, and they find hate easily fills their noggins. Although I am the goddess of emotions, I find this perverse obsession deeply disturbing."

"You're the goddess of hate." Hercules mocked Aphrodite from his stall, simultaneously performing a loud fart followed by a satisfying snort, laughing with his deep laugh. "They are doing what you want them to do like I just did. *Emoting!*"

"No, *no!*" Aphrodite protested. "That is such an unbecoming name for me, but what can I expect from a mere mortal? Such a lack of respect, I should blight thee with the emotion of loneliness!"

"Too late for that, missy," Hercules said and laughed.

"Oh, what the—" Aphrodite was being jostled and pushed away from the door, and she emoted her dissatisfaction.

Fortunately, Eros's innocent ears could not hear the last words in Aphrodite's exclamation since it was unbecoming for the goddess of emotions.

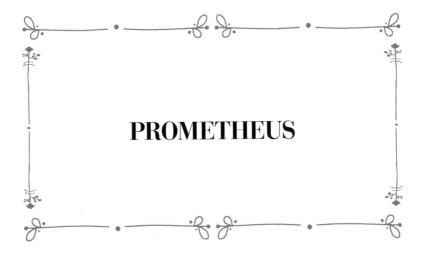

# PROMETHEUS

The jostling of pigs took some time. Zeus was the biggest pig, and when he decided to move, the rest of the pigs had to adjust to his desires. If Zeus shuddered, the rest of the pigs would twitch as his movements rippled through their bodies. As Zeus circulated around the sty, another pig named Prometheus eventually appeared at the door.

"You seem very dignified." Eros mollycoddled every god now because gods and goddesses appeared to like being pampered. Real feelings about a god or goddess didn't seem too important as long as others appreciated them. A bit of smoke or a string of fat sizzling, wafting heavenly aromas? Gods really do not want much.

"Me? Nonsense!" Prometheus stated with a bluntness that Eros was not familiar with, at least not in relation to gods. "You're not getting any advantage over me with vain compliments. I am what I am!"

"Sorry." Eros was uncertain how to proceed with this god.

"No problem, young sir," Prometheus assured. "I won't hold it against you."

"You are a god?" Eros ventured cautiously. Before with Zeus and Aphrodite, asking questions was discouraged, but this god demanded a different approach.

"I am Prometheus, a titan, and the god of knowledge." This god's response was promising.

"Knowledge?" Heartened, Eros tried another question. Eros's expectations and emotions rose commensurate with his hope. Maybe Prometheus, the god of knowledge, could answer all his questions.

"Why yes, I brought knowledge to all the creatures," Prometheus reminisced, responding to Eros's unspoken question. "When I brought fire from heaven to earth, I brought the knowledge of life and death to all creatures, pigs, dogs, and even humans."

"How about horses?" Hercules whinnied in the background.

"Horses are too stupid to know what knowledge is," Prometheus responded without hesitation. Eros got the feeling that he was in the middle of an ongoing repartee between the horse and this particular pig. "There is an ancient human story about how Adam and Eve ate an apple from the Tree of Knowledge, the original forbidden fruit. That is a lot of malarkey! What is a fruit going to do but make you fat? And that is what is happening to you, Hercules, with all those end-of-season apples you are getting."

"You're eating 'em too," Hercules said, bickering.

"But an apple from the Tree of Knowledge?" Eros wondered aloud. "Shouldn't that have some special attributes?"

"Humbug! An apple is an apple regardless of what you call the tree. Like money, knowledge does not grow on trees!" Prometheus was pretty firm on this. "Knowledge gained is due to learning, not eating!"

"And this makes you special for humans?" Eros was grasping for answers, trying to keep up with Prometheus's logic.

"Yes, I am humanity's best friend. They know me as the god that brought fire to them, raising them out of their primal condition." Prometheus paused, making sure the pup was paying attention. "The truth is that I brought them the fire of consciousness, allowing them to seek truth and accumulate knowledge, which in turn was used to light many flaming fires to this day."

"Knowledge?" Eros had so many questions.

"Knowledge is seeking and attempting to understand the transformative nature of ultimate reality."

"Am I supposed to understand this?" Eros asked.

"Before I brought awareness to humanity, humans were Aphrodite's slaves, wandering in a broth of directionless emotions. With my fire, the flames of knowledge have spread forth among pigs and humans, melting emotions like candle wax in a blast furnace, and it was I who brought this spark of knowledge to the world."

Proudly, Prometheus was enthralled by his own tale. Eros noted that dogs were left out of Prometheus's last diatribe, leaving Eros to assume that dogs were not blessed with Prometheus's fire.

"There is an ugly rumor that I was punished for doing this. I was not, but I was designated the god of politics, which is really Athena's bailiwick, since knowledge unleashes sentient beings in proximity with other sentient beings to mercilessly manipulate knowledge into forms that are beyond recognition."

"Athena?" Eros was duly impressed, although he was not quite sure why. According to Prometheus, he wasn't sentient enough to know why.

"Being smeared by Athena's dirt, politics has been associated with me so much that I am now the figurehead. Isn't this punishment enough!" Prometheus complained. "As I have told many others over the millennia, my allegory for being the god of politics is like being chained to a rock and having my liver eaten from my living body by day only to have the liver replenished overnight. Then the birds of prey feast upon it the next day and the day after that and so on. Politics is my eternal punishment!"

"But isn't politics the maintainer of the avenues to the pursuit of happiness?" Eros questioned.

"Does this mean you are the traffic cop of happiness?" Hercules quipped from his corner, keying off Eros's question.

"Yes! I have written the declaration of happiness," Prometheus responded to Eros, ignoring Hercules's satire. "And parts of this declaration have appeared in the American Declaration of Independence!"

"Really?" Eros would have been stunned by this comment if he knew what the Declaration of Independence was.

"All pigs are equal. They all have inalienable rights, the chief right being the pursuit of happiness! Obviously, an idea of happiness for a horse is a lump of sugar."

"Et tu, Prometheus! Friend to humans, anathema to horses." Hercules feigned being hurt.

"Naturally, humans butchered the translation, but that was to be expected." Prometheus sighed. "In fact, humans left out the next line in the *declaration of happiness*. 'Nothing stands in the way of a pig's pursuit of happiness, not even pigs.'"

Eros had a hard time accepting Prometheus's claims. Could it be that the humans actually got this right regardless of what the gods said?

As if to prove Prometheus's last point, Zeus started making a ruckus, and the pigs began moving once again. Eros's interpretation was that if you were the big pig, you had unlimited happiness and that any lesser pigs would get lesser levels of happiness. Before Eros could ask about this, Prometheus was none-to-gently pushed away from the door.

"Darn, just when I was going to ask him the rest of my questions!" Eros exclaimed. He avoided using bad words that he did not know yet by the whiskers on his muzzle.

# ATHENA

Prometheus's replacement, an elegant female, was jostled into view. Although she was jostled into place, thrusting her head into the screen of the gate, she made the transition look like she strode forward, and she purposely jammed her face forward in the most regal fashion. She gave the impression that every step she took was measured and understood before it was undertaken regardless of Zeus's gyrations on the other side of the pigsty.

"You must be Athena?" Eros was over his hesitation in asking questions. Like pups, each god is unique. "What are you the goddess of?"

"I am, young pup," Athena stated calmly. "I am the goddess of wisdom and science."

"I thought Prometheus was the god of wisdom?" Eros looked for clarification.

"He is the god of knowledge," Athena replied calmly. "You could say I am the goddess of applied knowledge. Of course, not all applied knowledge could be considered wise, but I can't account for the weaknesses of men or pigs."

"And science?"

"Prometheus takes in some weird stuff sometimes as knowledge." Athena cracked her calm façade with a small smirk. "Before you can apply knowledge, you need to know if the knowledge is valid, or you could get unexpected results from your application, which doesn't demonstrate any wisdom at all. You are a fool if you constantly seek unexpected results."

Athena's placid delivery was a relief after Zeus's arrogance, Aphrodite's bipolar display of emotions, and Prometheus pained presentation.

"Athena, you are so calm," Eros could not help remarking.

"There is a clarity in truth that cannot be found anywhere else. Humans call it reason, but truth is beyond human reasoning. Truth is! For the foreseeable future, the sun rises in the east. Because of its constant repetition, the action of the sun has been tested supremely, and the appearance of the sun every day is an established truth. Within this truth there is clarity and a calmness, and this serenity is the focal point of my being. Truth leads to the door of enlightenment."

"The truth is vague to me." Eros struggled with Athena's explanation.

"Of course, you're young and still learning to seek the truth," Athena assured him. "When there is truth, there is no argument— unless you are a politician, in which case the truth is irrelevant, subordinated by self-interest."

"That's interesting," Eros replied, not sure if he got an answer for his query or not. "Politicians?"

"Don't get me started," Athena protested, but then she ignored her own plea. "Over the millennia politicians have taken my truths and twisted them into weapons, and to my great dismay, I have been designated the goddess of war."

"How can that be?" Eros was disbelieving.

"Truth can be wielded into untruths! Untruths lead to misunderstandings, and misunderstandings lead to the weaving of more untruths until division, even war, is inevitable. There is no wisdom in war, only the arrogance of acquisition or the desperation of survival. The truth must not be trumped by untruths. That is true evil!"

"Isn't Prometheus the god of politics?" Eros asked.

"Mistakenly so, yes," Athena acknowledged. "But politics is an art form of applied and misapplied knowledge."

"Can I be wise?" This question burst forth from Eros's head. Although appearing to deviate sharply from their conversation, this question arose organically from the exchange, which was very interesting in a queasy sort of way. This led Eros to believe that truth may be the ultimate reality he was seeking, but untruths appeared to be the normal way of life. Would he be able to gather enough wisdom to find his way?

"Are you wise enough to answer that question?" Hercules cackled in the background, challenging Athena. The horse chuckled at the pig and the dog struggling with the squirmy subject of truth. "You are as bad as metaphysical philosophers! Don't know nothin'."

"You ask a lot of questions, and you don't believe everything you hear." Athena ignored the rude horse and considered Eros's question. "That's a good start, but I don't know what you will do with the answers yet. So I can't say. Wisdom is in the application of knowledge, not the accumulation of it."

"Oh," Eros suddenly realized that he had been dillydallying with the pigs for quite some time, and he became very anxious that he needed to get back before his mother was aware of his absence. He feared the truth of his existence would be extinguished if he was discovered.

"If you always seek the truth," Athena continued, "you may find wisdom."

"Sorry, but I've got to go. Athena, thank you!" Eros blurted out. But at that moment, Zeus decided he wanted to move again, and she was swept away anyway.

Eros literally hightailed it back to the house. His tail stuck straight up while he ran at full throttle, his little legs churning like the wheels of a locomotive. (His high tail revealed his anxiety since holding a tail up high while running is not normal for dogs.)

When Eros got back, Skylark was not in sight, so he scanned his surroundings. Way in the distant field, he spotted his mother rounding up Matt and Wanda, whose play had gone out to the far end of the market garden. Skylark was herding them to the house, and when she got back, she was not happy.

Sitting there, minding his own business, emanating vibes of virtue, Eros watched the returning crew. Leaving his mind as empty of thoughts as he could muster, Eros was seated on his backside, his two front legs straight in front, looking as innocent as could be.

"What have you been up to?" His mother knew Eros had not been as innocent as he wanted to appear, but there were no signs of wrongdoing for her to address. Having no evidence, she knew the scallywag was getting away with something. She just did not know what, and telepathy wasn't helping.

"Nothing," Eros replied effortlessly. He pondered, *"Does this make me a politician?"*

# MINGLES WITH MAKAI

E ros had to wait a week for his next opportunity. Skylark was not happy that Matt and Wanda had wandered so far away, and she had suspicions about Eros, so she was extra vigilant. Eros was quite pleased that he had avoided the spotlight of his mother's ire, yet he was anxious to visit more farm animals.

This day, Skylark decided in the late afternoon that she needed a nap, having been on duty for more than ten hours, watching those rambunctious pups since before daylight. Finally, his patience paying off, Eros watched as his mother nodded off and drifted into a fitful nap. Like a spring wound up for ten days and tightened for the last ten hours, the moment Eros thought she was asleep, he sprang like a mouse-trap going off.

Eros had seen the horse and been in the barn. Now he was looking for sheep. He knew where Hercules and the pigs were; however, the location of the sheep were a mystery up to now, and he didn't like mysteries. The last place they could be that he could think of was behind the barn opposite Hercules's corral. Unseen by the normally observant horse, Eros raced around the right side of the barn, and by golly, he was right. Using the side of the barn at one end, the sheep paddock was framed with light fencing, wood posts, and a single wire surrounding a large area filled with grass.

Eros slipped easily under the fence, an electric fence. He was unaware that he had just slipped under a live wire. He ran up to the five sheep, which were clustered at the far end of the enclosure. As he neared the sheep, Eros slowed down so that he could slowly walk up to the biggest of them.

"Hi," he said with a cheery voice.

The five sheep eyed the dog warily. They were aware that even small dogs could bring annoying barks, disturbing their meditations while they were chewing their cud. Unbeknownst to humans, sheep know the difference between domesticated dogs and wild dogs or wolves, so their response to sheep dogs, for instance, was not because they were afraid of the dog or feared being bitten but because of the disturbances to their meditations, which most domesticated dogs bring with their yapping. Sheep believe they are a thoughtful bunch, even when their thoughts are vacant.

"Who are you?" There were four white sheep and a black one. This question arose from the one sheep larger than all the rest of the white sheep.

"I'm Eros, a pup from the house," Eros replied. "And you?"

"I am Makai, the majestic." The sheep raised his stately head. "King of kings!"

Eros did not say anything, but he thought that Makai might be a bit pompous.

"I've heard of this fantastical place, the house," the big sheep replied. Eros realized that the sheep's fenced-in area was behind the barn and did not afford a view of the house. For the sheep, this unseen house philosophically was both mythical and theoretical. "That is supposedly the location of paradise."

"Why, it is!" Eros confirmed, thinking of the kitchen, which they called paradise.

Makai grumbled to himself, not sure if he could believe this... dog. Eventually, Makai returned to the conversation from his internal mumblings. *Or perhaps that is my stomach rumbling,* Eros thought in response to his mingles with Makai.

"So you must know our god, Zeus?" Makai asked and challenged simultaneously.

"I have spoken with Zeus," Eros confirmed, but he was uncomfortable with throwing around the term god.

"You must be a demigod!" Makai surmised.

"No, no," Eros quickly shot that idea down. "I'm just a puppy."

"Ah, a modest messenger," Makai concluded.

"Who are you guys?" Eros inserted one of his own questions, shamelessly trying to deflect the conversation away from the idea that he was a demigod. He had enough on his plate just being a dog.

"My flock is an assortment of found and lost sheep," Makai replied.

"Are you a found sheep?" Eros was struggling to understand the distinguishing aspects of each type, lost and found.

"I am neither. I am the representative of the god of gods, and I am what needs to be found," Makai informed Eros. "The lost are those that have strayed from my path and don't agree with me."

"If you are not *lost or found* but something else, then there are three types of sheep in your flock?"

"I am a liminal creature, chosen and anointed by the gods," Makai answered as if he had practiced this response. "I am not part of the flock. I exist in a reality beyond."

"You look like you are here?" Eros was confused again.

"I appear as the god of gods wishes me to appear," Makai explained.

"And the others?" Eros decided this line of questioning did not have an end, and so he went back to the here-and-now questions stacked in his repertoire.

"Melissa is the svelte female over there." Makai pointed his nose in the direction of one of the female sheep. "She doesn't feel it is politically correct to be heavy, so she doesn't eat a lot. She is also passionately devoted to the flock operating democratically, something that is patently absurd."

"Marty is the young male farthest off." Makai raised his nose in Marty's direction. "He thinks I am old school, a might-makes-right type of leader, whereas he feels scientific application of new political techniques is better. It's all nonsense! Also, he is hoping to unseat me as the head sheep. So he is delusional as well!"

"Uh-huh." Eros did not know what to say to this.

"The god of gods has given me this position. So with God's grace, I was given the power to minister to this poor flock." Makai paused to emphasize the wisdom of his words, but Eros was not sure what wisdom he could find.

Eros was just listening and observing, so as silence followed Makai's pause, the sheep rushed to fill the silence.

"Myrtle is the beautiful, fat female who lives in the comfort of following my every word," Makai said with a definitive, proud voice.

Oddly, Eros could not distinguish between Myrtle's fatness and Melissa's thinness. As far as the little dog could tell, the rest of the sheep were all the same size and shape. Other than the black sheep, he couldn't tell them apart. Excluding the larger Makai, all the white sheep looked identical. He was only able to differentiate them by smell.

"She doesn't worry about proving my word right or wrong. If it is my word, science be damned," Makai continued, ignorant of Eros's musings as he proudly proclaimed, "Myrtle is not lost. She has found me!"

"Mirabelle, is the last female, the black sheep. She is the most lost soul of the lost. She has no beliefs, and she lives to question mine. She is an empty shell since she does not believe in me. I ignore her existence, except, of course, when she goes into heat, and she services my needs, even though she does not want me. Might has its privileges!"

Eros was aghast, but he was just a puppy and didn't know anything, so he stood mute. From Eros's perspective, he felt it was not right for a male to force himself upon a female. His rudimentary knowledge of this subject (from his mother, naturally) required the male to obtain consent before going forward with sex.

"Forcing yourself on Mirabelle? Isn't that wrong?"

"How human you sound!" Makai taunted.

"I'm not human!" Eros complained bitterly. This was an insult of the highest order to the young puppy, but it also cracked the image of humans as always being stupid. In the case of rape, which Makai was describing, Eros viscerally felt that humanity had it right and that this sheep had it wrong.

"God gave me these females. My duty is to satisfy God's wishes." Makai laughed at the awkward puppy. Subsequently, he explained the situation. "What God wants is by definition right!"

Makai was content with his explanation, but Eros was not.

With a start, Eros felt he should be getting back. Somehow, he felt a telepathic touch whenever his mother started to dream about him, and her dreams of Eros tended to wake her up. Anxiously, he bid adieu to Makai and began his return before he was missed.

Makai's position on politics and life had nothing to do with Eros wanting to leave his presence, but Makai's opinion of sexual relationships changed how Eros viewed this particular sheep. Eros felt sleazy, even dirty after talking with Makai. *Are humans not as bad as everyone says they are?*

Between Prometheus's view of the Declaration of Independence and Makai's blindness in regards to his sexual philosophy, Eros began having his doubts about human badness.

In keeping with his insistence on continually asking questions, Eros asked, *Is the art of doubting at the heart of gaining knowledge?*

# MAKAI

Upon Eros's return, Skylark awoke just as he settled into a seated position. Eros had been successful with his *I know nothink* ploy, and his mother, upon waking, remained unaware of his latest outing; however, it was a close call.

A couple of days later, his mother again fell asleep, and Eros bolted for the sheep paddock. At the electric fence, Eros could see that Makai was off to the side, working a choice knoll with a recent growth of grass to chew on.

As Eros passed Hercules on his way to the far side of the barn, the horse realized that Eros was heading to see the sheep. The horse corral was large and extended past the near-end of the barn. Hercules turned and trotted to the back end of his paddock.

From a particular vantage point in his paddock, Hercules's panorama passed by the pigsty, which depending on the direction of the wind, offended his sense of smell, but he also had a full view of the fenced-in area of the sheep. As long as he could withstand the odor of pigs and sheep, Hercules could see everything, and as it turned out, he could also listen to everything due to his remarkable hearing.

"Beautiful day," Eros greeted Makai, noting that there were no clouds in the sky. On this early autumn day, the temperature was in the seventies.

"God gives us days like this," Makai responded. Every one of Makai's thoughts was *God this* or *God that* in a roundabout fashion.

"Zeus is your god, correct?" Eros inquired because he knew very little about religion. "Can you tell me more about your god?"

"Why, Zeus is the greatest god," Makai replied without hesitation. He knew what he thought he knew, and there was no prevarication in his knowledge, right or wrong. It is very comforting to not worry about what you don't know, even if your prospects for gaining new knowledge are drenched by a reign of ignorance.

"You mean Zeus, the pig!" Although Eros knew the answer to his own question, he still was astonished that a pig could be a god.

"And his consort Aphrodite!" Makai proudly declared.

"Could you say you believe in Zeus with all your heart?" Eros attempted to summarize Makai's relationship to his god and goddess. "He represents ultimate power?"

"I do," Makai proudly replied, which disappointed Eros. The pup was looking for the complex and got the simple. Makai answered the question but gave no details.

"And?"

"Zeus personally anointed me leader of this flock!" Makai pompously raised his head, looking down his nose at the little dog.

"You mean he peed on your feet!" Hercules sarcastically whinnied from his corral. Although distant, the horse's message was clear.

"Undoubtedly, yes, holy urine blessed me!" Makai looked up from his nipping of the grass and chewing. "I try to emulate everything that Zeus does. Heaven is in the barn, and God's perfection rules everywhere!"

"Heaven is in the house," Eros protested.

"You are naïve, young puppy!" Makai decided to educate this little dog. "Heaven is where God is, and Zeus is in the barn!"

Sullen, Eros questioned his own knowledge, not knowing that this was a sign of wisdom. The puppies only had a vague idea of the upstairs of the house, but maybe Makai was right. Maybe! (If this was the way to wisdom, why was Eros so uncomfortable questioning his own knowledge?) To his dismay, Eros found he was questioning his own questioning. *Does this mean I am not just wise but wiser?*

Knowledge gets associated with your identity, and when your knowledge is questioned, you are threatened. The impact can be profound if you discover your knowledge is wrong. Some call this state *confusion*, others *chaos*, but either can be stressful. Later, a wise dog once told him to "embrace the profound because that is where true knowledge can be found." Eros was not that wise yet, and he felt this experience was disconcerting. Or was it Makai that irritated him?

"Of course, Zeus has manifested in the barn." By repeating his point, Makai chided Eros with a patronizing tone as if he were talking to a child with diminished intelligence. "I try emulating Zeus whenever I can. Zeus knows all, hears all! Maybe if I imitate Zeus enough, I will gain these attributes too."

Eros in his small experience sample rationalized what Makai was saying. Makai's universe was his corral and the barn, and the biggest thing in the barn was literally Zeus, the pig. (Zeus was not as tall but was actually wider and heavier than Hercules, the horse.) Lastly, Zeus's lifestyle and thinking resonated strongly with Makai, making him a Zeus wannabe. The reasoning was sound, but the rationale was weak.

"What god do you believe in?" Makai speculated, turning a penetrating stare at Eros as if he were talking to someone untrustworthy, a heretic, or worse, a demon. "If you don't believe in what I believe, you are a demon!"

"I don't know. I just met Zeus!" responded Eros. Quickly realizing where he would fall in Makai's cosmology, he decided to be amenable. "I guess Zeus is as good as any god."

"*Good!*" Makai was relieved. "I didn't want to stomp you to death."

Eros discovered it disconcerting to not tell the whole truth, but from Makai's response, he learned that the projected outcome of telling the truth would be more disconcerting. In hindsight, Eros had to conclude that he had been wise in not doing so, but he was conflicted. Wisdom that requires lying at times does not make sense.

"Oh," Eros sighed and concluded to himself. *Hypothetically, everyone speaks truths and untruths. The challenge to find the truth is to navigate between these two paths to discover a way to the true truth. So even when it is in front of everyone, how can dogs (or people) find their way? Wisdom lies hidden in plain sight, even when the truth cannot be found.* Eros felt that he was losing wisdom with every thought he had.

"How can creatures ever find their way?" Eros telepathically spoke this out loud.

"Every way leads to Zeus, young pup, and this is *the Way*," Makai recited as if he were reading from a script. "Place your trust in God, and God will place his blessings upon you—unless he wants to teach you a lesson."

"What happens then?" Eros was intrigued.

"You are damned and sent to hell for absolutely no justifiable reason!" Makai declared. "I don't know for what, but Apollo, a god like him, was damned and sent to hell at the whimsy of Zeus. No one has seen him since!"

"Didn't Apollo go to Mount Olympus?" Eros thought back on his recent conversations with Zeus.

"Oh, yes!" Makai shuddered, confused. "Ah, I was just testing you, young puppy. You listen well!"

Here we are with a truth and an untruth. *Did Apollo go to heaven or hell?* Given Eros's experiences with Zeus's personality, which embraced inconsistency, ironically, he figured both truths could be true.

"God seems to be one bad dude," Eros ventured an opinion, leaning toward Makai's version of the story, including damnation.

"Hush, don't say such things," Makai warned. "Zeus may hear you, and off you may go!"

"Yes, this whimsy of God can be dangerous," Eros concluded.

"Absolutely!" Makai declared loudly as if Zeus were listening to their conversation, and he may have been since Zeus, the pig, was at the outside barn door, surveying his dominion.

"But, if Zeus knows all?" Eros reviewed their recent ruminations, which his quick mind did normally, and he stumbled on a conundrum. "Then God already knew I would say what I said. In a way, God put these words in my mouth, and he has required that I say them to you."

"*Egad!*" Makai screamed and started running in circles on top of the grassy knoll, nose to the ground as if he could find some new facts in the dirt. "God is testing me! Did I pass? Did I fail?"

"I have no idea," Eros confessed. Makai was a sight, running back and forth, stopping to nervously shoot out a stream of pee. As the shooter on the grassy knoll, all Makai could think about was conspiracies. Eros offered a path. "Maybe you should ask Zeus?"

"Yes, you're right," Makai looked down at Eros. "But are you part of the conspiracy?"

"What conspiracy?" Eros was a bit mystified, and in his next breath, he answered his own question with a question. "You mean me asking questions makes me a conspirator with God?"

"This is a conspiracy to test my faith," Makai cried. "I believe! I believe! *I believe!*"

"I see your dilemma! Asking Zeus if you passed is tantamount to a declaration that you don't believe in Zeus!" Eros intonation turned the statement into a question. "And stating that you believe belies the truth that underneath it all you don't believe, else you wouldn't need to state it."

"No! No! *No!*" Makai said in denial.

"So if you ask Zeus, you are doomed, exposing your lack of belief, and by not asking Zeus, you never know the truth, leaving you living in doubt, which is as good as being doomed? This is a test at which you can't succeed!" Eros posited out loud these hypothetical conclusions to his cogitations. "Since I see no other options, I assume that you fail the test. Regardless of what Zeus says, you would be forever uncertain that you were still Zeus's champion on earth."

Makai's analysis of Eros's logic was superseded by his emotions, and the sheep was stunned by this mini explosion of reason. Regardless of its flaws, this hypothetical truth and implied reality disturbed Makai. Suddenly, Makai stopped chewing his cud, looked around desperately, and then bolted to the far side of the sheep's corral bordering the barn and the outdoor pigsty gate.

Sheep are contemplators, but they are not known as intellectuals, so this barrage of ideas overwhelmed Makai's comprehension, demanding him to choose between two impossible choices for him, and so he chose abasing himself with Zeus.

Off he went trotting as fast as he could toward the pigsty. Looking back over his shoulder, Makai cast a glaring glance at Eros so powerful that it should have turned him into a pillar of salt if it had any magic. From Makai's reaction, Eros concluded, *If you can't resolve the dilemma, it is best to ignore the crisis.*

Since Makai had left, Eros realized that his time was up with Makai anyway. Eros bolted back to the house and was just able to settle down when his mother awoke from her nap.

"My!" Skylark remarked. "You have been so good lately!"

"God must be on my side," Eros declared. The problem was that Eros didn't know which god. To himself, he thought, *Maybe I really should say, "May the Pig bless me!"*

# MELISSA

With a level of confidence setting in that the pups had been trained not to stray too far, Skylark's naps became a regular occurrence. For his part, Eros almost made a science out of predicting when she would fall asleep and wake up. Once Skylark's head nodded three times and dropped, Eros was gone.

The next morning started as a bright autumn day. The temperature had changed dramatically overnight, and so it was crisp and cool outside. The leaves on the trees hinted that they were about to change, with colors peeking out from cracks in the green foliage.

To a more jaundiced eye, these colors were muted earth tones, but for Eros, these festive leaves were swaths of reds, oranges, and yellows, brush strokes painted across the horizon above the newly mowed pasture and the distant roadway.

The colors were alive with activity. Around the farmyard were several trees, which were adorned with jaunty hanging chandeliers. The sky was bright blue and the air crisp and cool as Eros trotted past and around the end of the barn.

Oddly, Makai was at the far end of the sheep's corral, and he would remain so through all of Eros's subsequent visits. Makai was avoiding Eros, and in his naiveté he could not understand why. During this visit, Eros encountered Melissa moseying about the patch Makai had occupied yesterday, and although lush with grass, he inexplicably vacated today.

"Hi, Melissa." Eros always started with a chipper if unoriginal comment.

"I'm Mel," she responded with a friendly but mildly apprehensive manner. "But I am not sure I should be talking to you. You upset Makai terribly!"

"I didn't intend to," he replied. "Should I go over and apologize to him?"

"No, he doesn't want to have anything to do with you," Mel responded after thinking about it. "He needs to calm down, but when I see him later, I'll let him know about your apology."

"Thanks," Eros meekly replied.

"With this apology, I guess I can talk with you," Mel continued, gazing adoringly toward Makai. This was the first time that Eros had ever encountered love between a male and a female. He had known of love between a mother and a child, but neither Mary nor Skylark had relationships with partners like this that he knew of, so this was a new experience. (Mary had a male friend named Ted, who visited with her in heaven, yet this sense of love was not present.)

"I love politics." Mel broke the momentary silence.

"Politics?" Mel had jarred Eros back to reality. "Does this mean you don't tell the truth?"

"Oh no," Mel laughed. "Politicians tell the truth when it suits them. The best lie is the truth stated the right way. Believe me!"

Unfortunately, Eros was innocent, but he would learn later in life that when anyone told him, "Believe me," he should never believe a word out of their mouth again. Since this knowledge had not yet dawned on him, Eros was totally vulnerable to anything Mel wanted to say to him.

"Just like now?" Cooed Hercules, who as usual had sauntered over to the side of his corral to listen in and offer unwanted advice. "So did you tell Eros the truth or a lie?"

"Be quiet, you old glue bucket!" Mel replied none too politely. Hercules chuckled. He loved it when he irritated the sheep or pigs, and Mel's response was indicative of his success. The more impolite her response, the deeper his chuckle would be.

Although this repartee had given Eros a bit of time to think about what had been said, her logic drove him to silence since it defied his comprehension.

"To politicians, lies can be truths, and truths can be lies. Your reasoning is impeccable in a twisted way, but I'm not sure that I can twist that way," Eros admitted.

"I see you are a young pup, so let me just tell you the way of the world." Sheep are not remarkably heavy thinkers, but Mel danced around Eros with intellectual cleverness, enjoying the fun of confounding the inexperienced youngster. "Everything boils down to politics, and politics is the art of governing. Forget all the isms. The primary political form of all governments starts with oligarchy."

"Oligarchy? What is an oligarchy?"

"Yes, good. You're a smart little pup." Mel propped up his confidence, raising Eros's head with her nose while the little furry beast was lost in thought. "Politicians are charlatans. They try to sell you something you don't want by convincing you that you do want it."

"How is that oligarchy?"

"Most politicians are from the richest people in the land. An oligarchy is when the *crème de la crème* of a country, the richest of the rich, rule the country," Mel began her diatribe. *Sheep do like to talk a lot!* Eros thought. "Oligarchy is when the rich are considered the smartest regardless of whether they are or not, and they are given whatever they want. It's like Makai with the flock or Zeus in the pigsty. Zeus goes to the trough first and eats and eats and eats until he is about to burst. Then Zeus's consorts follow, doing the same thing, all the way down until the last. By definition, the poorest and dumbest in the society gets the crumbs."

"But what if the poorest aren't stupid?" Eros questioned, wondering if Mel was lying. Or was this truth stated the right way so that it became a lie? Or was it the truth that was actually true? Dumbfounded, Eros desperately wandered through this garden of thoughts and could only find weeds.

"Of course they are stupid." Mel was surprised that Eros was starting to muster some real questions. "You have to be really daft to want to be poor if you are smart."

Eros was not worldly wise, but he innately knew that circumstances could change the course of one's life regardless of one's intelligence. This is the thought at the heart of the Way of the dog. Conserve your cleverness and focus on surviving so that you have the most acumen available to find happiness when the opportunity arises.

Eros struggled with the concept of intelligence. Matt was no intellectual giant, but in the Wild, Eros would bet that he would be a genius at surviving. Conversely, Matt finding happiness would probably drown in his obsessive mental state focused on survival. Being smart smacked at one's relative position in the context of life and what the wisdom of that situation required. Eros could not see how cleverness was always supposed to be associated with wealth.

"Oligarchies have been dubbed in some societies as trickle-down politics or trickle-down economics." Mel went back to her didactic diatribe. "Obviously, in an oligarchy, the ideal is that nothing trickles down. But enough has to, or the minions may become *difficult*."

"Do humans have oligarchies?"

"Oligarchies are universal, my boy," Mel assured him. "Because they are not as intelligent as animals, humans have one problem. While animals have the sense to stop eating before they burst and to allow some stuff to trickle down, people just blithely keep on eating until they blow up. Trickling down be damned!"

"Oh my." Eros was upset, imagining an image of Mary blowing up like a balloon and exploding. Mary was good to him, and he cared for her; however, he recognized that she did eat first and that the dogs got the scraps with the less savory dog food.

"You have to call it what it is. Oligarchy is the ultimate of pure greed. This is the natural state for all living things, which cannot be denied!" Mel concluded, very satisfied that she had educated this puppy. "Oligarchy is a beautiful thing! You can't believe how beautiful it can be...for the rich."

*Oligarchy is God's ultimate order?* This thought puzzled Eros, who felt Mel embraced a crystal clear picture of Zeus as God through Makai's vision of him, but her devotion to Makai prevented Mel from thinking any further.

Eros wondered, *If the universe is infinite and God is the universe, then God is infinite? If so, shouldn't everyone strive to see further, beyond rich or poor? Isn't the goal of everyone to search as far into the infinite as they can? Shouldn't anyone want to see their god in their own way? Not someone else's way? With this focus on rich and poor, does this belief in oligarchy just demonstrate a disbelief in the infinite magnificence of God?*

Eros could not answer any of these questions.

"By the way," Mel concluded, preparing to move to a greener side of the corral. "Don't talk with Marty. He is very, very bad!"

"Why?" Eros asked, mystified.

"He doesn't agree with me," Mel simply stated and walked away.

Eros wandered back to the barnyard, dazed and confused. Oligarchy was the supreme order of the universe? He couldn't believe this to be true, or maybe he didn't want it to be true. Mel's thinking sometimes went into deep thoughts, but at other times she was shallow like water pouring off a red-tile Spanish rooftop.

Today, the water splashed off the roof but then swirled down the gutters quickly.

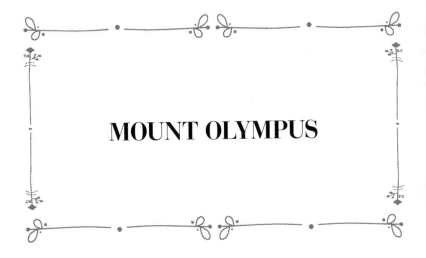

# MOUNT OLYMPUS

J ust a hair under four months after their births, the puppies noticed a great deal of activity around the barn. Aphrodite, who had been growing steadily, was moved to the empty stall adjacent to the pigsty, and there she delivered six piglets.

Athena cooed with happiness for Aphrodite, applauding the birth of such healthy pigs. Prometheus simply noted the event with scientific interest, but Zeus saw things differently. If the gate between the pigsty and the stall had been opened up, he would have happily entered and eaten every piglet one by one until they were all gone. His desire to pursue this cannibalism was so strong that it permeated the ambiance of the barn, making it awkwardly unpleasant for the rest of the pigs.

This situation of new piglets created a crisis for Mary. She was aware for some time that the pigsty was getting too small. With the arrival of more pigs, some piglets could be sold or given away to good homes, but there were only so many good homes in the neighborhood. She would need to keep some. Mary pondered this dilemma for several days.

On the third day after the piglets' arrival, Mary tied the puppies up outside. Mary preferred that the pups were outside, if possible, every day over being in the kennel because the cleanup was easier. When she did this, all the puppies were aware that something infrequent if not unusual was going to happen, like a truck delivering bags of dog food.

This was a relatively rare occurrence, but it did give the pups a front row seat on whatever was going to happen in the barnyard. Whether a delivery or bringing the horse out of his corral for Mary to ride on, the little dogs were arranged side by side and tied to stakes around the barnyard close to the house, where they could see everything.

Today none of the normal farm chores were on the docket. The little pack was accustomed to events happening at the barn on these occasions soon after they were tied up, but this was not the case today. There was no activity for the longest time. With front row seats, the puppies were lined up in a row and waited patiently for the show to start. They started to realize that this event was atypical.

About seventy-five minutes after they were tied up, a big white box van arrived, turned around, and backed up to the barn door. Two workmen got out, pulled out a ramp, and attached sides to the ramp. Mary was talking with them, instructing the men on how to proceed. Once the ramp was ready, the three humans disappeared into the barn.

There was a lot of oinking and squealing from the pigs, but then there was a moment of quiet. Mary started by calling soothingly, trying to calm the beasts in the barn and convince them that nothing was wrong.

"Zeus, baby!" she cooed, coercing him to come forward. "I have some nice apples for you!"

Mary appeared with an apple in hand and a couple more in her arms. As she backed out of the barn, Mary was followed by Zeus, who loved apples.

"Hallelujah, *Hallelujah!*" Zeus squealed in glee, recognizing the truck. "My time has come! I am off to Mount Olympus!"

"Zeus, you fool!" Hercules commented. "Don't get in the truck! They are going to take you to market!"

"Nonsense. I cannot die, you lost soul!" Zeus informed him. "I am a god, and I am immortal. I am off to Mount Olympus to join Apollo and to wallow in the glory of the heavenly pigsty!"

"*Don't get on that truck!*" Hercules whinnied as loud as he could, snorting many times for added effect. "You'll be slaughtered!"

Zeus did not heed Hercules's warning. The temptation of apples and the promise of glory were too much for the god of gods. Mary's assuring tone of voice added to Zeus's comfort level. *Mary has brought me up from a piglet. She would never betray me,* Zeus assured himself.

When Zeus's backside disappeared into the truck, the men closed the back gate of the truck to prevent Zeus from backing out. The men quickly disassembled the ramp and packed it up. Then they got in the truck and departed. During their maneuvers, words on the side of the truck came into clear view. They read, "Mount Olympus Meat Co."

After the truck left, Mary stood in the yard, crying. She was attached to the piglet that she had raised. He grew up to be a fine pig; however, life on the farm required change, and support of the farm required sacrifice. The same was true with the puppies! She loved each of the new puppies, but they had to be sold to support the farm and her modest lifestyle. Dogs are not the only ones who must be stoic.

"Feels very much like the Way of the dog." Eros felt this sadness and Mary's counterbalancing rationale. While Mary was very emotional, he could not fully read her mind clearly, so he filled in the considerable gaps and mused.

"Sacrifice and survive today for happiness tomorrow!" Skylark affirmed.

Scratching behind his ear with his back leg, Eros couldn't understand why Mary was crying. After all, Zeus had gone to Mount Olympus, which was his greatest desire.

"Oh!" Eros had an aha moment. Eros concluded, "Those must be tears of joy!"

"That's the Way of the dog," Skylark interjected this thought into all her puppies. "But Mary is not a dog."

Eros was confused.

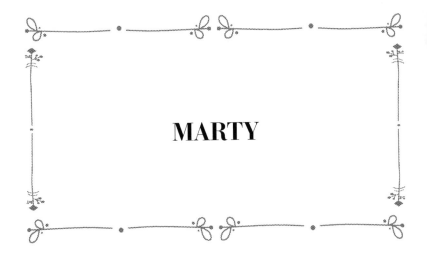

# MARTY

ecause of the scary political vision Melissa presented, Eros was afraid to go back to talk with the sheep, and he cowered near his mother when he could. Mel's discussion had left him disturbed that anyone could see the world as callously as that, but he eventually concluded that the universe wasn't always filled with dishes of milk and soft chunky food served in paradise.

Eventually, Eros's confidence grew enough that the day after Zeus's ascension, he ventured back to the sheep's paddock after Skylark fell asleep. This time the gloomy-faced Makai and supercilious Melissa were at the far side of the paddock, chomping merrily on the greenest grass in the corral, leaving Marty and Myrtle sauntering nearby on a previously cropped area.

*Trickle-down economics in action!* Eros thought, commenting on the division of resources as he trotted over to Marty. Although he couldn't visually tell the two sheep apart, when he got closer, he could smell the difference. Their smell was like a fingerprint to him, totally unique for each individual.

"Hi," Eros started with his jaunty greeting, but there was an undercurrent of apprehension. Eros felt nervous and tense, which was uncharacteristic of him. *The Melissa effect,* he concluded. Eros could easily ignore Makai's physical jittering, but Melissa's thoughts on truth terrified him.

"Hi, Eros! I'm Marty," Marty responded with a smirk. "I hear that Mel has been filling your head with a totally cynical view of politics."

"Er, yes," Eros confided, not quite sure what cynical meant.

"Not all politicians are heartless salesmen, and her oligarchy theory is hogwash! Literally!" Marty replied by giggling, which turned into a full-throated laugh. It appeared that Marty found humor wherever he could, especially pigsty humor. "Pigs? Hogs?"

Marty laughed uproariously, but Eros didn't get it and looked at Marty quizzically. As Eros would come to understand during the course of this conversation, Marty loved to laugh heartily over his own inane jokes or puns, sometimes uncontrollably. Marty's laughter began to ease Eros's anxieties.

"Oligarchy is just another term for nature, such as human nature, pig nature, sheep nature, and stuff like that." Marty grinned. "Politics is really about controlling an oligarchy, not pandering to it. All the political systems have their different methods—democracy, communism, socialism, and others, but the control of oligarchy is the premier feature of all advanced politics."

Marty's was a different approach than the other sheep's. Eros brooded over Makai's and Mel's philosophies, his mind a boiling tempest. Their beliefs sounded reasonable, but inherently, they seemed unfair to Eros. Marty's sounded right, but these political philosophies didn't sound rationally possible or practical.

"Do they work?" Eros braved a question, but his face was still bleak. The birth of cynicism was burgeoning upon Eros countenance, flowing like a black river across his consciousness.

"Of course they do. Well, to varying degrees!" Marty confidently maintained. "Democracy is a sterling example where the rich are constantly held in check. Power to the people!"

"And pigs can fly!" Hercules joked from his corral.

"That's good, Hercules." Marty had a good, solid chuckle, and although Eros was reserved, he continued to respond to Marty's cheerful attitude. Marty's jokes were useless, but his good humor was infectious.

"I'm with Hercules on this. Isn't a government holding the associated oligarchy in check just a fantasy?" Eros's dip into the river of cynicism made him question his innocence and Marty's assertion. In this context, hope was just a sticky Band-Aid being pulled off a wound. "Isn't Mel right?"

"Nature cannot be denied. Men and dogs cannot help but be corrupt, yet this tendency can be controlled!" Marty continued earnestly. "Why do you think God gave out brains? For example, you have a river that overflows its banks, causing destruction and death. If you can control that river by building a dam, wouldn't you do so?"

"How would this work?" Eros opened his mind to the possibility that something would be better than Makai's and Mel's visions.

"The two-party system is perfect," Marty continued blithely. "The nation comes first, and the moderates on both sides work together to get the optimum solutions for all issues. The nation's interests come first, and the political parties are unimportant."

"Sounds perfect," Eros stated. "Too perfect!"

Eros questioned whether Marty's positive nature was taxing the boundaries between his idealism and reality. Eros did not feel qualified to contradict Marty's contentions, but these claims made him wonder about Marty's state of mind. The line of demarcation between idealism and delusion is very fragile if it exists at all.

"All these governments are like scientific tests showing the efficacy and weaknesses of each government, and with great communication and bipartisan creativity, all these issues can be resolved promptly, selecting from the best available options. And each supreme leader, president, or prime minister is the humblest and wisest person in the land."

"You're definitely delusional!" Hercules bellowed from his paddock. "You're going a bit hog wild!"

"I see what you're doing. Hog, hog wild, ha-ha!" Marty was starting to make Eros uncomfortable as he laughed wildly, embracing Hercules's comment as if it were one of his own jests. After a while, Marty calmed down enough to continue. "Good one, Herc! Love those puns! Do you have any questions now that you know what real politics are about?"

"Do all politicians lie?" Tentatively, Eros was regaining his confidence. This query was a good sign, signaling that Eros was finding a new normalcy, returning to his relentless penchant for questions.

"All politicians are pigs in a poke." Marty again laughed at his own poor joke. "You never get what you expect, poking through the gate."

This time Marty thought that this was so hilarious he couldn't stop laughing for several minutes. Not understanding the humor, Eros waited for Marty to settle down, but there was an odd infectiousness to Marty's unbridled enjoyment that affected Eros. Eros's rock-hard tension had cracked, and he couldn't help smiling at Marty's antics. He thought, *I wish I could express my emotions so freely.*

"So far, what I have heard about politics is scary," Eros divulged.

"The scariest politics are human politics." Marty finally controlled his laughter enough to respond. "But political science will help to solve all the problems by removing the corruption and bringing us to a perfect pan-society discussion, which humans call their national discussion. If you boil off all the steam, the essence of politics is this national dialogue."

"Political science fixes everything? National dialogue? Sounds like you are selling snake oil." Eros's cynicism lingered as he wondered where he came up with this analogy. *Snake oil?* At times,

Eros was still mystified by where all his thoughts came from. He guessed a lot of peripheral, irrelevant information was coming from Skylark (or others) during his mingles. Fortunately, some of these random thoughts became occasionally useful.

"The national discussion is the social plain where free speech is allowed, and the free press and free media are insured, from which the truth must be weaned. There is nothing more sacred to a political system, oligarchy excepted, than being able to ferret out the truth from this national dialogue." Marty took on the look of a glassy-eyed idealist staring into indeterminate space. "A true patriot would hold the national discourse as sacred!"

"Mel says everything is an oligarchy," Eros struggled to summarize what he had learned. "You say that all the forms of government are geared toward preventing or reducing the effects of the underlying oligarchy and that the essential tool of these forms of government in this primal political conflict is the truth that arises from the national dialogue?"

"Yes, by golly, you've got it!"

"I've got what? I feel I have been twisted so much that I've turned into the Gordian knot." Eros didn't know what a Gordian knot was, but he felt like one.

"You've been hog-tied!" Hercules quipped from afar.

Missing Eros's question, Marty obsessed on Hercules's comment, pouring gas on the sheep's pile of jokes fire. Naturally, Marty found this last comment hilarious and laughed uncontrollably.

After a while, Eros concluded that Marty might not stop laughing in the immediate future. However, time was passing, and wisdom instructed that he get back and pretend he had never left Skylark's side.

When Eros bid adieu to Marty, Marty was unable to respond, and Eros was unsure if Marty heard him. Eros wondered if Marty's laughter was spawned by humor or hysteria. This question, which could be extended to all political scientists, is one of the mysteries of the universe.

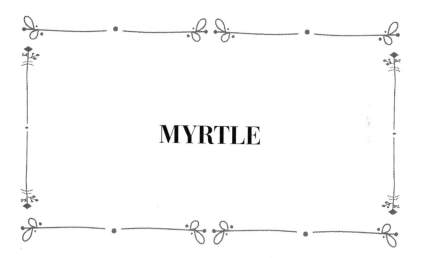

# MYRTLE

Skylark was becoming very predictable. Although seasonably cool, his mother would curl up and fall asleep near the house's doorsteps, luxuriating in the heat of the midday sun. On the day after his visit to Marty, Eros was off when his mother's nap commenced. Galloping past the barn, Hercules spotted Eros's streaking body as he zipped past the right side of the barn, and he ran up to the nearest sheep that he had not yet interviewed, Myrtle, swerving past Marty to get to her.

"What do you want?" Myrtle was startled, her mental voice raised up a pitch, fear showing on her countenance, and flight due to fright was a distinct possibility.

"Oh, I'm sorry," Eros apologized. "I got carried away. Running is so much fun!"

"Well, I never. *I never!*" She emphasized the second "I never" with an indignant tone, nose pointing straight up in the air.

"I am truly sorry for frightening you," Eros repeated his apology.

"Don't do that ever again!" Myrtle was pouting now as much as a sheep could, tail sticking straight out. Sheep didn't often stick their tails out like that during normal conversation if hardly ever, but Eros had successfully received such a response.

"Hi, I'm Eros." He attempted to change the subject while starting the interview at the same time.

"Well..." Myrtle grumbled for a bit.

Eros hung his head dejectedly, hoping to show shame and remorse.

"I'm Myrtle," she mumbled after making Eros wallow in humility sufficiently enough to soothe her feelings. Eros rationalized that Myrtle wanted to inflict an equal amount of emotional pain on him in proportion to the amount of pain she had felt at his abrupt arrival.

"I've been talking with most of the sheep about their views. I'm just an ignorant puppy, and there is so much I need to learn. Can you help me?"

"Maybe," Myrtle said, starting to relax.

"I'd really appreciate it!"

"I believe firmly in God, but I am a firm believer in science too." Myrtle's anger was starting to thaw. With this softening, she was doing a lot of affirming.

"I'd love to hear your thoughts," Eros encouraged with a smile. The other sheep liked to talk, and hopefully, this observation was universal among sheep and would remain true for Myrtle.

"God is everything, and everything is God!" Myrtle stated strongly.

"You believe in Zeus, the god of gods?"

"By heavens, no!" Myrtle was set back a bit. "I am a scientist. God is one and indivisible, an unseen force for doing good on this earth. I believe God is female, and she cares for me, and looks after me."

"Do you believe in any other gods or other things?" Eros plowed forward.

"I just believe in God. I don't clutter my beliefs with sins and all that other stuff like humans do," she assured him. "Dirty distractions, I call 'em!"

"Interesting," Eros contemplated this unforeseen turn of events. This was the first time he came across a god that was not represented in the barn or Mount Olympus.

"You can't see God, but she is there! You can't feel God, but she feels you and for you!" Myrtle appeared to be reciting something as she gazed at a cloud in the sky.

"You deny reality exists so you can say your god exists?" Eros asked, curious.

"That's not what I said," Myrtle responded defensively.

"Your god exists but can't be seen or heard or felt," Eros stated. "So how do you know your god exists? And if your god exists in a place outside of natural reality, doesn't that question the existence of natural reality?"

"I believe she exists! My belief is impervious to the illusions created by mind or matter!" Myrtle was getting unpleasantly aroused again. This female sheep blurted out uncertainly, "And—and God is natural reality!"

Although Myrtle vowed belief, the desperate timber in her voice shouted out her disbelief in what she was saying. Her evident disbelief in her last statement seeped into the mood of their conversation.

"Okay, okay! God exists!" Eros assured her. "Let me ask this then. Being a scientist, how do you know she exists?"

"Why, the Great Book tells me so!" Myrtle brightened up.

"The Great Book?" Eros had never heard of this book before.

"Yes, the Great Book tells the great story of life and contains everything about the universe, about how to live on this earth, even how to worship God. *The Book of the Dog* is just a tiny sliver, a small chapter out of the Great Book. Even the sacred books of humans like the Good Book are in the Great Book. Everything is in this book, and if it is not in the book, it doesn't exist."

"Everything?"

"Everything!" Myrtle's confidence was unbreakable.

"All knowledge?"

"Yes, *Everything!*"

"That's a whole lot," Eros deliberated. "Knowledge is changing and limitless, right? And the combined knowledge of all the creatures on the earth is limited, correct?"

"I guess so." Myrtle was sensing that uneasy feeling come up again, similar to the feeling she experienced when Eros had almost run into her like a crazy dog.

"What if something is not in the Great Book?"

"Then it doesn't exist!"

"But if it did, how—"

"It doesn't exist, plain and simple," Myrtle interrupted him.

"So how is this scientific?" Eros was now puzzled.

"I can test any hypothesis against the Great Book!" Myrtle declared triumphantly. After a pregnant pause, she continued, "Don't you know the scientific method?"

"Yes, I've heard of it," Eros wondered how a little puppy could know all of these things and theorized that it came from one of the numerous history and science news stories on the television that Mary watched. His memory was starting to mature and perform better the older Eros got, and Eros concluded that these thoughts stuck. He decided the gift of an excellent memory was a nice thing to have—sometimes. "Let's take a recent example. Human scientists discovered four new elements a few years ago."

"Yes?" Myrtle did not understand where Eros was going.

"Someone, some entity updates the Great Book?"

"The Great Book is complete and perfect!" Myrtle replied. "No need to add anything to it to make it more perfect. That's silly!"

"So it is unchanging?"

"Yeees," Myrtle drawled out the word, suspicious of Eros's intentions, wariness dripping through her response.

Eros was trying to think this through as he summarized what he had learned from Myrtle. "If knowledge is changing and unlimited and the Great Book is unchanging and a compendium of animal knowledge, which is limited, how can it contain everything?"

To Eros, this was an innocent question, but Myrtle took this quite differently. Eros looked at knowledge as analogous to a little ball he played with in the house. The ball is rubber with a white background and brightly colored pictures of sailboats on both hemispheres. The center of the ball has an azure slash across the ball's equator, representing a blue body of water, on which the boats bobbed up and down on.

As Eros played with this ball, he would perceive pieces of the ball as little vignettes, and questions would arise freely while the ball bounced all over the place. Even the ball itself would generate questions as it escaped his grasp and bounded away, trying to hide from him when Eros tried being the alpha male. Like the ball, Eros's idea of knowledge was a toy to be tossed in the air and played with, while perceiving and understanding were coincidental.

"I've heard from the others!" Myrtle exploded. She obviously didn't look at things the same way that Eros did. She stamped. She swooned and moaned and hollered incomprehensible words in anguish. "You take our words and screw them into unrecognizable twisted thoughts! You turn our worlds upside down! You are a *demon*!"

"What's a demon?" Eros recalled having heard the term before when talking to Zeus, but he had never had the opportunity to ask questions about this fantastic creature before.

Myrtle huffed and puffed. "A demon is someone who not only disagrees with God and her representative, me in this case, but also connives to confuse God's representatives!"

"What if my questions are just exposing an underlying confusion that you are immersed in and can't see?" Eros's last question did not go over well, and it didn't take a fortune-teller to predict that he was going to be foiled in getting an answer.

"Arghhh!" Myrtle twisted her face in a grotesque pout and turned red with anger. (Being red-faced is virtually unknown in sheepdom, since the red has to glare through a sheep's white [or black] wool coat.) Scientifically contemplating this phenomenon was not in the cards for him as Myrtle charged Eros, trying to butt him and shouting, "Die, demon! Die!"

Although startled by the turn of events, Eros instinctively leaped, avoiding the rock-hard head of the oncoming sheep.

"Die, dog! Die!" Myrtle stopped in a cloud of dust, turned, and prepared for another charge. *"Die, demon! Die!"*

At this time, Eros thought it prudent to end the interview. He turned and ran! He ran twice as fast as he had earlier in the day in order to get away from Myrtle, and when the two of them came to Marty, Eros slipped between Marty's legs, while Myrtle had to swerve around the male sheep. Even as he ran, he could not help but ask questions and search for answers, even though this repartee was locked in his brain.

*I've seen this anger before,* he concluded to himself. Zeus came foremost to his mind. Why did Zeus and Myrtle get so angry? I was just asking innocent questions. Aren't all questions innocent?

Initially, Myrtle was hot on Eros's heels, but she was a good-sized sheep who rarely ran more than ten feet. *She can't match my nifty speed,* Eros thought to himself. With that said, she was surprisingly fast, slowly catching up to the shorter legged puppy.

Soon Eros cleared the corral's fence with Myrtle huffing and puffing right behind him. As he slid under the fence like a baseball player sliding into second base, Eros perceived Myrtle screeching to a halt, dirt and grass flying everywhere. Eros heard a zap as Myrtle touched the wire fence with her nose. Eros turned and looked at her.

"I'm sorry." He tried to comfort Myrtle, but she would not be comforted. She wheezed and grunted and pawed the ground, pacing back and forth behind the electric fence, snorting wildly. The electric shock only added to her frazzled state of mind, making her go berserk. Eros was sure that Myrtle would be ripping her hair out in chunks if she could make her hooves work in that way.

"Why are you so angry?" Eros asked, but Myrtle was beyond answering. Eros grasped for an answer. During Skylark's presentation from *The Book of the Dog,* she opened a portal to allow the pups to access the rest of the book. Even though Eros preferred to be in the field, he looked into the dogdom portal once in a while. Unexpectedly, this situation evoked a memory from this book, which calmed his mind.

# Maybe

Maybe there is a secret place in every creature that is sacred to their understanding of the universe.

Maybe when this sacred place is shown to be inaccurate, the creature feels its understanding perishing.

Maybe when these beliefs die, they shatter and explode like light bulbs on the hard pavement of life.

Maybe when that creature realizes this phenomenon is occurring, it lashes out in profound grief.

Maybe the being is not aware that when a sacred understanding ends, this is not the end but a new beginning.

Maybe in the intensity of this emotion being emoted, the creature pulls bitter denial close to its breast.

Maybe the beast cherishes this denial, hiding the truth from itself, clinging desperately to a false pretense.

Maybe denial is like a python, its coils wrapping around the victim's heart, suffocating the host.

Maybe the being panics as it feels the perception of the glory of reality collapsing and they are afraid.

Maybe we are all beasts in the field, pretending that we know reality when in truth we know not.

Maybe we have forgotten the wonder of the world and the universe and need to strive to remember again.

So many maybes! We must answer these maybes many times in our lives with the courage to seek truth.

Or the maybes turn into an apocalyptic vision of devastation, and our hope dissolves into desolate desperation.

As he turned from Myrtle and headed home, Eros thought about this entry from *The Book of the Dog*, wondering if he had the answers, and concluded, "I don't know. I'm just a little dog. Maybe one day."

# MIRABELLE

**E**ros was smarting and not in a good way. He was shaken from his encounter with Myrtle, and it took two days before he regained his composure and thought of going back. Summoning the courage to return, Eros had to wait patiently for Skylark. (It's easy to be patient if you are afraid of what you want to do.) Today his mother was fidgeting, making it difficult for her to settle down. Skylark felt as if there was a shadow hovering over their happy life, but she couldn't figure out what was bothering her. Finally, she did sleep, and he did go.

Eros ran as normally as he could toward the barn and the far paddock, but it felt like his legs were moving in cloying quicksand. Running up to the electric fence, he surveyed the corral. Fortunately, Myrtle was at the far end, while Mirabelle, the last sheep he wanted to interview, was luckily nearby. As he hesitated to slip under the electrified wire, Myrtle looked up and locked eyes with Eros. A stream of unmitigated hate emanated from her. *Does this mean that Myrtle loved me passionately per Aphrodite's theorem?* Eros thought.

He cautiously slipped under the fence, watching Myrtle. She did not move, so Eros proceeded vigilantly, checking Myrtle's position often. His obvious fear was that Myrtle would come upon him unaware and attack, but in the end, Myrtle put her head down and continued grazing, deciding that Eros was not worthy of further attention, not to mention a hundred-yard dash.

"Hi, Eros," Mirabelle broke into his thoughts. "I'm Mirabelle, but I am sure you know that."

"Er…" Even though he was distracted, Eros was a bit surprised at this. His practice was to begin the introductions himself, and he was a bit off balance.

"You can call me Mira, and I understand that you want to know what I think. Is that correct?"

"Yes," Eros hesitated, paranoid. He checked where Myrtle was. Since she had not moved, Eros came back to Mira's friendly face and marshaled his questions. This resulted in a bit of hesitation, but Mirabelle smiled and waited.

She was a fine female sheep, but with one fascinating feature. She was black. So too, she exuded a down-to-earth nature as if she were Mother Earth personified. The corral helped support this ambiance, especially with the smells of earth and manure, surrounded by grass and mud and trees in the background.

"Which god do you believe in?" Eros got started. All the other sheep believed in one god or another, so this seemed to be a natural question to start off with.

"I don't believe in any god," Mirabelle responded. Her smile was infectious, calm, and tinged with a sense of humor, even though she never tried to be funny. "I believe in the Universe, and I believe that the Universe is a holistic entity that is trying to communicate with us."

"The universe?" This was an unexpected admission. The little pup attempted to process this information, but the process was not working. His brain had gotten used to having a god or gods cluttering the countryside. For him, this sudden diversion was mind-boggling.

"The wind in the trees is trying to tell you something. So is the water in the river, the snow when it falls. I believe in Everything, not in the distilled visions of entities comprised of part or all of a vision of Everything, which in turn manifests as various flavors of the perception of God."

"Whoa! You're going a bit too fast for me," Eros admitted.

"And I try to learn as much about Everything as I can," Mirabelle continued with her quiet but jaunty delivery, a smile on every breath. "I know so much that I know I know so little."

"Everything?"

"Eros, you are just like me," Mirabelle went on. "You have an insatiable thirst for knowledge and the courage to pursue it. You are just at the beginning of your journey, but your journey will not end with me."

"I'm not going anywhere."

"That is debatable." Mirabelle seemed to know more about the ways of the world, and she probably knew that Eros would not be at the farm much longer; however, this was not the point of her discussion. "Regardless of where you are physically, the journey I am talking about is the journey of your mind…and your soul. There are so many philosophies, so many religions. There are so many intellectual realms for you to wander through!"

"You go, girl!" Hercules hooted from his paddock. Mira's smile broadened a bit at Hercules's comment, but Eros just ignored the horse.

"I don't know any philosophies." Eros started to wonder who was leading this interview.

"You need to open your eyes." Mirabelle stared directly into his eyes. "Typical! You don't know the name of your current philosophy. The philosophy of dogs is mostly about stoicism. Do you understand half of what this philosophy is about? *Probably not!*"

"Mama is telling us!" Eros blurted out defensively.

"And she is doing a good job!" Mira smiled. "But when she is done, you're not done because you learned just one philosophy. There are so many other philosophies to learn from. Whether you believe in this one or that one or none of them, following what you want to follow is up to you."

Eros was fascinated but still overwhelmed.

"I fear this will be the only time that we meet, Eros, so I need to tell you more than you want to hear," Mirabelle continued. "I believe in magnificent dualities in the universe, male to female, mother to child, and the most majestic duality that I know is Everythingness to Nothingness."

Now Eros was fully flabbergasted. The feeling he experienced was a huge weight on his back, and the weight consisted of all the ideas in the world. Overcome, Eros sunk to the earth, his legs splayed outward in different directions.

"These are mirror reflections like the endless multiple dogs you saw."

"You have seen my vision from the bathroom?" Eros asked. "You believe me?"

"I have seen what you have seen," Mira assured him. "I have mingled with many types of animals and made a discovery. After the gift of life, everyone has a gift to bring to life. My gift is mingling skills far superior than most animals on the earth. This is how I was able to see your memories."

This was very comforting to Eros. Finally, someone believed him.

"But we must return to describing how to learn about ultimate reality. I believe in the windless wind passing over eternal fields of golden wheat under a cloud-filled sunset, the rays of the sun playing upon the wisps to give a panoramic light show of reds, oranges, golds, and purples. This universe is glorious!"

Eros had progressed from overwhelmed to stunned.

"Whoever you are, you are at the center of your own universe." Mirabelle continued to take the lead. "And this existential perception must be cherished. The majesty of Everythingness must be embraced so that you can experience the splendor of Nothingness. Then you can perceive the whole from the parts."

"Are you done with your spiritual mumbo-jumbo?" Hercules neighed from his paddock. "You're going to give this pup a headache."

"I speak what I feel, Hercules," Mirabelle replied with a smile. "You might try it sometime!"

"And I might feel like eating hammers and nails," Hercules hooted back. "But I guarantee that I won't like it."

Mirabelle didn't take the bait. She wasn't going to get pulled into a conversation with Hercules. She just chewed her cud with a Mona Lisa smile adorning her face. This response was the most irritating for Hercules as Mirabelle gave back what she got without giving Hercules what he wanted.

Contrary to Hercules's concern, Eros felt a strange fascination at meeting a sheep that knew nothing and everything, but Eros could not yet tell if this was a vicarious thrill or a visceral dread he was feeling. Mirabelle's countenance comforted him, so he was leaning toward the former feeling rather than the latter.

"Right now, Eros, you are in the wasteland of knowledge. You know way too little to know what is up or down, right or wrong. You will feel lost, but if you really trust in the Universe, you will find that you are no longer lost."

Skylark had been dreaming fitfully. She had dreams of Eros running this way and that, with her trotting endlessly after him. Her dreams became disturbing as if her mother's instinct knew that Eros was not there, and this was what woke her up.

Her sleep interrupted, the first thing Skylark did was look for Eros, and she quickly confirmed that he was not there. She was not surprised, but she did become alarmed after she scanned the field and the horse corral. As far as she could tell, Eros was nowhere to be found.

She bounded out of her curled-up sleeping position and raced for the barn, letting her instincts guide her.

"I can stop being lost by attaining knowledge?" Eros asked.

"You must seek knowledge to find knowledge," Mirabelle parried. "Knowledge is endless! The Universe will guide the knowledge that you learn, and eventually, your identity will emerge. This happens when you are committed to the way of the Universe, whether through a god of your choosing or through Everythingness. You will no longer be lost, but you will be in the process of being found."

"And I'll just stop being lost forever?"

"You can regress when your commitment to either knowledge or the Universe wanes." Mirabelle's presence fairly glowed. "Everyone's commitment wanes at some point, but returning and recommitting to commune with the Universe brings unfathomable joy."

"Hmmm." Eros natural analytical thinking was stirred as questions started to arise. He had so many questions that he didn't know what to ask first.

"Appears your journey is going to end...for today," Mirabelle said and grinned. "Your mother is on her way, and she is spitting fire and brimstone.

"Uh-oh!"

# THE LAST LESSONS

J ust before dinner that night, the pups and Skylark congregated in the room called paradise, waiting to receive their bowls of food on the linoleum floor. Sounding a doggy trumpet, Mother yipped to get the attention of her minions.

"I'm getting food!" Mary anxiously replied. As usual, the woman misinterpreted Skylark's message.

"There will come a time when you think you can control everything," Eros's mother began, fixing an icy stare at Eros, who cowered under that cold heat. "And a time when you know control is a fantasy. I brought you up from baby pups to the young puppies you are now, and I controlled everything about you, protecting you as much as I could."

Skylark paused and looked intently at the other pups, only to come back and transfix her eyes on Eros, who was pretty quiet with downcast eyes. His encounter with his mother that afternoon still reverberated over his psyche, leaving him unusually submissive. Although pensive, he was acutely aware that his mother's subject of control was related directly to his actions earlier that day.

"As recent events have unfolded," Mother bemoaned the admission, "I have come to the realization that I can no longer pretend that I control all your activities."

"What?" Eros looked up.

Mother looked at all the pups after making this statement. All the pups were trying to keep up with Skylark's thinking, but Matt was scratching his head with his hind leg, obviously not getting it at all. Being cunning doesn't mean you are smart.

"You are all now strong and fast and ready to go in different directions." Mother hesitated because it is hard to admit you have limitations. "I have come to the realization that I can't keep up with all of you all the time anymore."

"Mama, Mama, I'll be good," Artemis spoke up, and the rest of the pups chimed in with the same good intentions.

"No, you will not," Mother said and lolled out her tongue, exposing a dog smile, looking at Eros. "You have grown into juveniles, and in some cases, you are already bigger and faster than me. Some of you can jump higher than me too."

Everyone knew that Eros could jump higher than any miniature poodle. This had become common knowledge. Charley was bigger, and several of the pups, including Eros, were faster than their mother as well.

"In other cases, you may become wiser and smarter than me." Mother looked at Artemis this time, and surprisingly, she then looked at Eros again. "But all of you will have to make your own choices. I need to give you the last lessons, which you must learn to accept a greater understanding of mingling in the future. There is more to mingling than what I can teach you. The last lesson deals with the dog's mantra."

This was puzzling for the pups since they had no knowledge of what she was talking about.

"You're too young to fully understand, but one day you will, hopefully." She paused. "As you know, we talk telepathically, and at times you have gathered more from my thoughts than my telepathic messages, or in other words, our minds mingled. This is what I have been doing for all of you all along. We talked, and I would sometimes impart words or meanings to help you continue the discussion. But there is more to mingling than that. I can actually imprint thoughts in your brain without talking."

"Huh?" This telepathic response arose simultaneously from all the pups.

"Yes," Mother confirmed. "I am going to plant a whole bunch of thoughts in your minds, and they will appear as if they are memories, as if you knew them all along. But this can be a bit startling for you the first time. So are you ready?"

Skylark looked at her pups dealing with their confusion. One by one, they acknowledged that they were as ready as they would ever be. Mother took one last look around. "This is the dog's mantra."

## Dog's Mantra

1) Everyone needs help. Don't be too afraid or too proud to ask. This is what the pack is all about.

2) The key to social integration is the ability to listen and the courage to allow quiet to exist. *Listen to the quiet!* If you don't, you will listen only to the sound of your own voice. The monotony of one voice shrinks your curiosity so that you fear acquiring new knowledge, and in doing so, you are no longer growing your own garden of knowledge.

3) Don't be sucked into someone else's nightmare, someone else's fears. Share your courage, not your fears! Fears are the alertness required for survival, but fears emanate

from the individual. By taking on someone else's fears, you redirect attention from your own fears and possibly away from your own survival.

4) Everyone wants to look up to someone. They want a leader to be admired and respected, one who takes their fears away. To be a leader, one must be ready to take on this burden. If you choose a leader, you must take care to question your leader constantly, reconfirming over and over again that he or she is worthy of your trust. Trust is not a one-time occurrence or a one-way street. Choosing a leader makes you responsible for whom you have chosen.

5) There are two basic aphorisms in life: "Don't be afraid," and "Be courageous." Don't back into life. Boldly drive forward! You are the *hero* of your own life. Realize that it is courage and not a lack of fear that one is striving for, and as the hero in your own story, you are worthy to do this striving. You do not need your parents' or friends' approval. You only need your own approval.

6) Life is like a river, and you are a little boat. Whether president or pauper, you are not and never will be in complete control. Life takes severe swings, ups and downs, but our directive is to survive. Between every crisis, there will be moments, some shorter or longer, where happiness can thrive. Be ready to be happy. Don't succumb to the mindset of survival.

7) Survival is dependent on knowledge. The more you know, the better chance you have of avoiding trouble, and if trouble happens, you have more options on how to get out of trouble. If food smells bad and you know it smells bad, your knowledge can inform you so that you don't eat it. If you eat bad food, your knowledge about eating grass and forcing yourself to vomit can save your life.

8) Learn as much as you can, but you must never stop learning, which can be very difficult. Old dogs can learn new tricks, especially if their survival depends upon it.

9) Have the courage to tell the ones you love that you love them at least once a day. You never know when you will part ways or the Big Nap will come upon you or your beloved.

10) We all come from and go to the Big Nap. There is nothing to fear in the Big Nap. However, the passage to get there can be troublesome. If you do go to the Big Nap, just remember the love that you have given. When you go to the timeless Big Nap, this love will envelop you forever. So love well in your life, for it is all you will have in death.

11) Be happy! Life is a brief blessing, so enjoy every moment. Love as much as you can because the Big Nap comes upon all of us way too soon and on occasion, unexpectedly.

Mother ended her subliminal thought transmissions. "The mind mingling is over. Is everyone okay? The first time can be disorienting." Mother looked among her charges. Matt, in particular, was glassy-eyed.

"Matt, you need to focus on number six. You tend to just gnaw on surviving like you are chewing on an old bone. The mindset of survival comes naturally for you, but it can prevent you from being truly happy. Happiness is not just surviving but being happy in between those moments."

"Charley, number seven can be your problem. You are such a wonderful doggie, but from time to time, the tip of your nose is all you can see. There is a whole world of predators that can come at you from all sorts of angles. To survive, you must learn and learn more and finally learn to use that knowledge to be alert to all dangers from all directions. Never stop learning!"

Turning her attention, Skylark focused on her female pups.

"Artemis, you are so empathic that number three is your biggest bugaboo," Mother continued. "You are so much the classic mother, but your empathy will every so often overwhelm you with another's fears or the shadows of fear, namely sadness. You will lead with your heart but maintain your courage as a shining shield. Embrace number five, and be your own heroine, Artemis!

"Wanda, you are the jokester among my pups, but now and again, that humor can hide your feelings," Mother softly chided. "Pay attention to number eight! You need to have the courage to stop hiding behind your jokes and tell people that you really love them! No joke."

Mother turned to Eros with a bemused smile.

"Eros?"

"Yes, Mama?"

"Eros, Eros," Skylark struggled with her thoughts. "I don't know what to make of you. You need to pay attention to every one of those laws, and yet in ways, you are more advanced than all my pups in all of the mantras. I went over the other pups' greatest weaknesses, but with you, I will point at your greatest strength. Keep asking questions."

"But you tell me to stop asking questions all the time?" Eros was surprised, "I know, but answering questions is tiring. I'm sorry that I get tired, but your questions are what make you *you*. In regards to the mantra, if you learn from your mistakes and learn to avoid future mistakes, this practice will not only help you to survive, but may even lead you to wisdom."

"How about us?" Wanda whined.

"Ask more questions, and see what happens. Anyone of you can achieve your version of wisdom. Whoever you are, I repeat, never stop learning, *yarp!*" Mother gave an unusual and untranslatable bark for emphasis.

"Was that a bad word, Mother?" Eros was shocked.

"That was the opposite of a bad word, Eros. Unlike humans, who say bad words for emotive emphasis, they have very few good words with the same emphasis. Dogs have a much broader and more precise language than humans in this regard, but don't get distracted with your questions now."

"Me?" Eros feigned innocence, but he knew what she was referring to, sensing his mother's uneasiness about their previous discussion on the subject of bad words. Skylark was warning him not to rehash their earlier exchange on this subject, which he felt that she still deemed fruitless.

"Your knowledge can fix everything in life as long as you don't get distracted. You must remember that, believe that, the purpose of life is to find happiness, and you can only discover happiness through the knowledge that you find."

"Here you go, Shyla!" Having heard Skylark's bark, Mary hurried to put down the bowls of food. "You've been real impatient today."

All the dogs, pups and their mother, smiled at Mary. They appreciated Mary for the food, but they loved her for her imperfection, which the woman shared with the dogs every time she misinterpreted them.

"For all of you," Skylark said, ignoring blithely Eros's not-totally-truthful response. His brief reply hid the truth that he was actually ready to ask just those questions that his mother did not want him to ask. "The eleventh mantra is the most important. I don't care if you are experiencing the worst days of your life or fighting desperately to survive. I want you to take a moment each day to savor the joy of being alive!"

There was complete silence as all the puppies were totally engrossed in this last lesson.

"I'm hurryin', Shyla," Mary responded as she put down a bowl of water.

"Now off with you scalawags, but remember—be a dog!" His mother scolded her pups lovingly. "Time for dinner!"

And it was time, as their tummies were starting to churn like little engines short on fuel, grinding slowly to a halt.

All the pups were profoundly influenced by these lessons, but Eros in particular felt his list of questions explode out of proportion.

He clung to what his mother had advised. He needed to learn how to use his knowledge to find happiness.

After dinner, he went to the kennel and lay down alone in a corner, and there, he thought and thought. He went over the dog's mantra that he had just heard in his mind as well as all the questions he had ever asked and all the answers he had ever gotten, and he came back to one thing he could do starting today...and every day—the one thing he identified that was totally under his control.

From that day forth, the first thing Eros did in the morning and the last thing he did every night was say how much he loved Mama and the other pups, even Matt. After a few days, he added Mary to this list, even though most of the time, the woman could not understand him properly. (Ironically, love was the one thing that humans did not misinterpret. Ignore, definitely, but if they allow themselves to accept it, people do understand love.)

As the days passed, the pups looked back at their mother as a prophet since all of the concerns stated in the mantras came true eventually, but being a prophet is easy. All prophets do is tell you that change happens, and no matter what, change always happens inevitably.

# THE DARKER SIDE OF THE WAY

A few days later, Mary brought four crates into the kennel and stacked them on the side. Eros wondered why there were just four crates since there were five pups, but he never got around to asking the question. "Not all questions get asked," Eros concluded.

The pups could feel their mother's apprehension at this development but also the conflicting feeling of resignation. She knew what was about to happen. She also knew that it had to happen.

If Skylark had litter after litter and none left the house, Mary would be like the old woman who lived in a shoe with poodles hanging out of every window. If you insist on bringing life into this world, you are responsible for that creature for the rest of their lives.

The pups did not grasp the changes that were coming and the need for those changes. The puppies just lived under the cloud of these ambivalent feelings. As the days went along, they forgot that the cloud was there and resumed playing and jumping.

One day, Wanda and Eros were having a particularly fine romp. Wanda would grapple with Eros and try to prevent him from getting some distance from her, and Eros would escape to leap high over Wanda. When Eros jumped, he was like a little fawn, soaring over Wanda, his legs out straight, pointing to the ground. Eros would turn with his bum up and his nose down between his paws, ready to spring. Wanda responded by twisting around, ready to meet Eros's pounce head-on. They knew each other's moves well.

The playing felt like it continued for hours, and they were so happy. Eros was on top and then Wanda, and then they would roll around, tussling and wrestling. As the struggle intensified, the two pups would test out their growls and snarls, and for a human looking on, they might appear to be really fighting; however, their telepathic connection was filled with laughter and joy. Today the focus was on the flow of these feelings, not the banter.

Unknown to the two pups, engrossed in their playful roughhousing, Mary entered the kennel and went straight for the two of them.

"Oh, Mary thinks we are fighting too hard," Eros stated, though he'd reached a superficial and incorrect conclusion. Misinterpreting a message is not limited to humanity; dogs can too! Because of their play, neither Eros nor Wanda understood Mary's intention. The excitement of the moment didn't allow telepathy to give them an accurate reading of the situation.

"Ah!" Wanda squawked as Mary scooped her up, walked over, grabbed a crate, and tossed Wanda inside. Moments later, Mary was on her way out of the door of the kennel.

"I love you," were the last words that Wanda said to Eros as she disappeared behind the door, and Eros knew there was no jesting in these words. Everything happened so fast that Eros didn't have a chance to reply. Within minutes, the rest of the pups became aware of Wanda's departure, and they were all trying to make sense of it. When the door to the house was opened for dinner, the pups rushed in, looking for Wanda.

"Where is Wanda? Where is Wanda?" Eros raced around the inside of the house, going in circles through the rooms. Eventually, when Eros realized that Wanda was gone, he felt a great sadness and collapsed in the kitchen, unable to eat his dinner. While Eros sat stunned, grief-stricken, the rest of the dogs ate in sullen silence.

Over the next two days, the white cloud of apprehension turned into the dark cloud of grief. Every time the pups went into the yard, they felt the shadow of loss pass back and forth, as if a shadow was flying over their heads. While the puppies cried, whimpering softly, Mary and Mother remained stoically calm, yet beneath that calm was sadness. Both Mary and Mother knew that this development was the best thing for Wanda over the years to come, but both had come to love this little bitch.

Shades flittered across the yard every day as the pups fell in heaps, grief-stricken with Wanda's departure. During this period of time, the pups would find a solitary place to lie down and contemplate what had happened, but their thoughts found no resolution.

Eros would learn that this feeling that Mother felt now was called being disheartened. (Erupting in his brain, the word brought a feeling that he did not like. It felt as if someone had surgically removed his heart.)

Eventually looking beyond this sadness, Eros missed Wanda's penchant for closeness during play and afterward when they would fall in a heap together, exhausted. These were memories of how they would commune together, savoring and sharing the happiness that they felt. Eros yearned for this type of closeness, and as the days progressed, he would sit next to Charley, Artemis, and Matt in turn. Although it was going to be a long road, they all started feeling better.

The yard, even the corral and barn, no longer appeared as interesting as before. Eros sorted through all his emotions, but after a few days, Eros remained troubled and sought out his mother.

"Mama? Mama?" Eros flagged her down. Since Wanda had departed, Mother did not talk as much to her pups. She was processing her feelings of loss just like them. Being older doesn't mean you feel less. In some ways, you feel more. Eros could feel a swirl of emotions mixing with her mingles.

"Yes?" Skylark stopped and sat down to listen. She sounded very tired.

A true stoic would not have approved of this emotional weakness, but in truth, the ideal stoic has never and will never exist. Creatures are creatures, dogs are dogs, and humans are humans! All have feelings, and these feelings cannot be contained by ideal intellectual constructs, only painfully constrained.

"I'm upset," Eros admitted.

"You shouldn't be!" Mother assured him, maintaining her stoical pretense of calm. "Wanda has gone to a good home. Why are you upset?"

"Because she was able to say she loved me as she left," Eros confessed. "But I couldn't tell her that I loved her before she was gone."

The downfallen little pup hung his head.

"I noticed that you have been telling everyone that you love them in the morning and evenings since I gave the last lesson," Skylark stated, impressed.

"Yes," Eros admitted, timidly.

"Did you say that you loved Wanda in the morning on the day she left?"

Eros thought and finally said, "Yes. We played until she was gone. Actually, other than our mindless banter, it was the last thing I said to her."

"Then you did say it," Mother concluded.

"But I didn't say it when she did."

"You were in shock, Eros," Mother informed him. "Your physical body puts you in a state of involuntary numbness to protect you. This is beyond your control, yet there is a lesson here that you can and should learn. Once you recognize you are in shock, you can guide your body and thoughts. On the river of life, shock is like a strong current. You can be overwhelmed and give up the helm, or you can guide your boat. Shock should not paralyze you as it did with Wanda; this is a matter of survival, and you must learn from this."

"She probably didn't hear me earlier in the day," Eros whined, not listening as well as he should.

"Believe me, Wanda will go over every day of her puppyhood in her mind and remember every detail, especially every minute on her last day with the pack," Skylark comforted him. "When I went on my journey to my first owner, I cherished all my memories from my puppyhood. Those memories were all I had from that previous time. And I recalled every word my siblings said before I left, even those they thought I didn't hear. I assure you that Wanda will remember you and what you said this morning."

Eros was comforted by this conversation, and he started feeling better. Continuing his practice of visiting each of his siblings, alternating day by day, the puppies began to share their sadness about Wanda's departure, and it helped them all.

Artemis even started her own alternating pattern, following Eros's practice, chatting with Matt or Charley when she was not communing with Eros. Pups are pups; they are resilient and began perking up, all but Charley, who was still in the dumps a week after Wanda's departure. Grief does not give up easily.

# THE DARKEST SIDE
# OF THE WAY

O
n a beautiful autumn day, Charley was plopped down in
the middle of the yard. Dust devils were twirling around
him on a cool but breezy afternoon. As Eros came into the
yard, he saw Artemis on the side with Matt, so Eros concluded that
it was his time to be with Charley. He moseyed on over and plopped
down, side by side with Charley, who was smack dab in the middle
of the barnyard.

"Whatcha doing?" Eros jovially began.

"Checking the perimeter," Charley replied. Although Charley
didn't go overboard, he had a penchant for the military mindset. He

had picked these terms up from Mary's boyfriend, Ted, who used to be in the army.

"You are doing what?"

"I'm on guard, protecting my farm," Charley stated flatly. "This is my yard, you know."

"Yes, I know, Charley!" Eros responded. Lately, Charley had been stressing his territoriality to Matt and Eros. Obviously, all their male hormones were expressing themselves now. "I've seen you pee all around it, marking your territory."

"Nothing in the north quadrant or the east or the west quadrants," Charley announced. He looked at the south quadrant, but since this included the house and the kennel, his westward review was cursory. "South quadrant is also secure."

"I understand Wanda is very happy with her new owner, an old lady with a granddaughter who visits every day." Eros relayed the most recent news. Their dog news was limited to the humans in their proximity. Mary was their single source of information, which was admittedly limited, but in regard to Wanda, she was a good source.

Mary liked to check up on her pups after they had been placed in families to see how the dogs and the people were doing. You could always hear Mary saying on the phone to the new owners, "If the pup isn't happy or you (the owners) aren't happy, bring that puppy back for a full refund."

"Yes, I heard," Charley acknowledged. "All's well that ends well."

Mary had a small bookcase filled with books that she would like to read, a couple of which were Shakespearean plays. Whenever Mary passed the bookcase and pondered them, she would look at them and dream of reading these plays. During these interludes, the pups could catch some of her thoughts as she read the titles off the spines of the books, murmuring them out loud. Charley found this particular line quite fitting with his version of the dogdom way.

"You don't sound happy for her," Eros said.

"I am, but I'm still sad. I loved Wanda." Like many military types, under the rigid surface, he had a sensitive, sentimental side, though it was usually paved over with asphalt. Last night he was blubbering like a baby as he bewailed Wanda's departure. When he finished, Charlie ate voraciously, finding comfort as many do. "All quadrants secure. I'm glad I'm back to work."

"Great!" Eros found that Charley was more at peace with Wanda's departure. Eros felt the deep shadow of grief was passing. Maybe that good cry he had the night before or the huge bowls of food he ate this morning had helped. "Wanna go with me to the corral and talk with Hercules?"

"Maybe tomorrow," Charley said, cracking the door of his depression. "Yes, I'll go with you tomorrow, but I've got to keep working today."

"Well, if you aren't ready to move off this spot, why don't we look at the clouds and the blue sky?" Eros said. "Always makes me feel better!"

"Nothing in the north quadrant...or the east or the west quadrants." Charley swung his head to look behind him to announce proudly. "South quadrant clear!"

"Aw, c'mon, Charley!" Eros exclaimed and turned over on his back, squiggling back and forth in the dirt, doing his happy upside-down wiggle. (Mary didn't approve of this maneuver since she had to wash the problem puppy afterward, but it felt so good!)

Eros was *shocked!* A large hawk was coming straight at him from the south! Eros imprinted the memory of this hawk in his brain. The hawk had a brownish-red head and a reddish-brown tail. With its wings wide open, the bird had a speckled white color under its wings.

*The shadows that have passed over the yard during these last few weeks are real,* Eros thought, but in the same instant he reacted, not thinking, with muscle memory. He twirled to his feet and leaped in one motion, and with his leaping ability, he escaped the range of the grasp of the oncoming bird. As Eros was in the air, he watched the soaring bird realize that her original target had moved too far off her line of descent for her to capture.

The hawk was searching for food for its baby hawks, its eyases, which had grown quickly and would soon be ready to leave her nest. Within milliseconds, Eros saw the hawk adjust her trajectory with a slight shrug of her wings for a new target in her line of sight.

"Charley, look up! *Run!*" Eros shouted. Charley was immediately alert, but his routine was to look north, east, and west. He did not look up!

Before Charley had a chance to look south, the big bird had sunk her claws into Charley's muscle and sinew right to the bone.

"Bark, *bark*," the yard erupted in barks. Even the horse neighed in alarm. Skylark, who had been napping in the yard, howled. Mary came running out, wondering what all the commotion was about, and when she saw Charley being lugged up into the air, she screamed.

Cracking twelve pounds, Charley was a solid load for this bird, so their ascent was painfully slow. Eros recovered from his escaping leap, and without thinking, he turned around and made a charging leap, hoping to grab Charley and pull him away from the hawk. Charley was not passive either. He was squirming and struggling valiantly, but he couldn't get loose from the hawk's viselike claws.

Eros made a heroic leap. He must have gone six feet in the air. He grabbed Charley's rear paw with his teeth. Regrettably, Charley's leg was moving so much that Eros's teeth skidded off. Eros fell to the earth with an empty heart. Looking up, Eros saw that the hawk and Charley had risen to about ten feet.

Frantic, Eros tried to think of what he could do, but he was helpless. Nonetheless, he jumped and jumped again until he was exhausted. Then he stopped jumping and looked up.

"I love you, Charley!" This was the last thing that was in Eros's control.

At about fifty feet above the ground, Charley stopped struggling. Telepathically, Eros could feel a tranquility come over Charley, an understanding of the poor options ahead of him and the acceptance that whatever fate awaited him was outside of his control. The valiant dog was as close to being stoic as any creature could get.

"You too," Charley clearly spoke to him, saying something to Eros he would never have said in any other circumstance.

Charley was not afraid of the bird, but he realized that if the bird let him go, he would likely not survive the fall. By now, Charley determined that the only option in his control was to wait and conserve his strength for the fight ahead.

As the hawk struggled to ascend, the two of them moved farther and farther away. The bird and dog were just two dark smudges about five hundred feet above the ground until they were just one dark smudge. Below that single smudge, the animals with the keenest eyes, Eros included, could see a little bundle falling precipitously. Charley literally dropped out of the sky. Slowly, the hawk spiraled down, following Charley's descent.

"He never looked up," Eros cried in his grief. This stupid thought was all Eros could think. Charley covered the quadrants, but he never looked up!

The immediate aftermath of the attack was a mixture of shock and grief. The façade of Skylark's stoicism cracked and then burst as she shrieked, howling in the greatest pain. Mary sobbed uncontrollably. Of all the pups, Charley was her favorite, and she planned to keep Charley for their home, explaining why there were just four crates. Following Skylark's lead, the remaining pups began howling too.

Not only is grief hard to overcome; grief is relentless.

# DEATH AND HAPPINESS

fter the hawk attack, the pups' privileges to visit the Wild were rescinded. Now they knew why there was wire mesh over the top of the kennel. The remaining pups mulled around the kennel the next day. Wanda's departure had cast a shadow of depression, but this shade gave way to the depths of despair as they descended into the shadows left after death.

Oddly, Eros was surprised to discover that snippets of happiness were easier to find. Artemis communed with him more often, and this brought him and her closer together. This new closeness brought Eros a new happiness that he did not expect. The proximity of Artemis's body reminded him of Wanda. He felt happy that Wanda was somewhere safe, and he was happy to have someone new to be near. Eros also found joy in remembering the times he and Wanda had played together.

Before he was a blank slate waiting to have memories impressed upon him, but for the first time, he started to go through these memories, selecting those and only those that brought a smile to his puppy dog mind. He discovered Artemis and Matt were undergoing the same transition.

Eros found out from Skylark that humans were inferior in this capacity. Humans could not control their memories, and they would dwell on unhappy memories, sometimes for entire puppy dog lifetimes, sometimes even longer. The fact was irrefutable. Humans hid their emotions from other humans.

Being telepathic, dogs must make an effort to hide their thoughts, and if strong feelings are involved, concealing a tempest of emotions is impossible. The effort is like trying to keep a sieve from leaking.

Comparatively, a depressed human is sad all the time and not fun to be around, or if the person is fun to be around, he or she is not truly having any fun. In contrast, dogs are part of a pack, even if they are estranged and separated by a thousand miles. Somehow dogs are able to share their emotional baggage, having a sort of built-in group therapy.

Dogs cannot understand why people have problems sharing their emotions. In turn, dogs try to help their human partners, but all a dog can do is love that person and work to siphon off some of the human's despair by being there. A dog would commit its whole being to dispelling the gloom of the human's sadness, whether the human knew it or not.

"Proceed with courage and hope!" his mother would say. "If you believe that hope is inextinguishable, then it is! Survive courageously—and that includes surviving sadness—and you will find happiness again. That's the Way of the dog!"

Even Eros's relationship to Matt changed. They went back to how they played as baby pups. Matt no longer went for his throat or bit to taste blood. They tussled and leaped and played like there was no tomorrow.

Soon, there was no tomorrow. Four days after the hawk attack, Mary came in, grabbed Matt, and put him in a crate. In an instant he was gone. The kennel was littered with several sleeping mats, and this time Eros noted that Mary grabbed one of the remaining mats for a bed inside the crate. Thinking back, Eros remembered that Mary had done the same with Wanda, but he hadn't taken note of this action at that time. So both Wanda and Matt had a little piece of home wherever they went. This epiphany gave Eros a glimmer of happiness.

"I love you, Matt!" Eros had overcome the impact of the shock as much as any pup could. From the hawk attack, he was praised for trying to save Charley. This praise felt empty, but his first leap to save Charley gave him confidence that he was doing better when dealing with shock. He also realized no one could ever overcome shock completely.

"I love you, Eros!" Matt responded to Eros's great surprise. They had fought so many times through some ugly and desperate battles, but in the end, Eros never really knew what Matt thought... until now.

Then, Matt was gone.

Unlike Wanda's departure, they were not sad at all.

"This is the Way of the dog," Mother said around the house and kennel. You could still feel a residue of sadness, yet her stoicism had a finality to it that was hard but also comforting.

Artemis and Eros consoled each other, but this did not last long. It didn't have to last long. The conflicting emotions of their loss and the happiness they felt about Matt finding a good home did not have to battle for very long. This time around, their happiness for Matt won out easily as they accepted that this was a much better fate than Charley's.

One day during this period, waiting for the next pup to depart, Eros sat down with his mother, deciding to go over everything he had learned.

"Mother," Eros said, but he didn't know where to start.

"Yes, my quizzical one?"

"I have learned a lot about the Way of the dog but also stuff beyond that, such as Everythingness and Nothingness. I have learned about the universe made of boxes, which you have told me keep getting bigger. I have searched, and I cannot find the edges and corners of the universe anymore."

"In the Wild, the edges and corners of the cosmic boxes cannot be seen," Mother confirmed. "Those places are beyond our knowledge and our imagination."

"Is that where Charley went? To a place where he cannot be seen?"

"No, Eros," Skylark replied pensively. "Regardless of the philosophy, no one really knows where that spark of awareness in any of us goes when we go to the Big Nap."

"Do you think that Charley is dead?" Taking a roundabout route, Eros voiced the doubts he was harboring.

"I don't know, absolutely," Skylark admitted since she had not actually seen Charley's body dashed upon the rocks. "But I am almost sure. I absolutely believe he died."

"Could he be alive?"

"No!" Skylark responded strongly, belying hidden emotions. "Hope is normally a good thing, but when it comes to grief, hope is a bandage that eventually gets ripped off, tearing the never healing scab with it. I cannot hope that Charley is alive."

Like Eros, she felt a nagging doubt about Charley's death, but her grief would not allow her to pretend that he was alive, for she feared that she would have to grieve his death a second time if she entertained the idea.

"I did wonder," Skylark admitted. "Because of our telepathic nature, dogs feel when one of us dies. The dog's personality is extinguished by the Big Nap. I did feel Charley's personality disappear. His transition felt a little different, but like every life, every death is different. I have no doubt that Charley is gone."

Doubt is a funny entity. It comes and goes. Sometimes you want it, but most times you are desperate to be rid of it. At this time, doubt loomed like a dark veil over the two of them, hiding what they could not see. Both dogs looked at each other silently.

"Can we talk about something else?" Skylark asked, breaking the spell.

"I have talked with the farm animals about politics and about how the world works, stuff not covered by the Way of the dog," Eros continued, obliging his mother's wishes, but he had not asked a question. Then again, he may not have known what question he wanted to ask.

"I am just a country dog. Religion and politics I leave to the pigs and sheep," Skylark finally commented. "All I know is the Way of the dog. Survival and happiness, isn't that all anyone needs?"

"I know there is more than that," Eros said. "I just don't know what is really relevant?"

"If your life becomes difficult and survival is your goal every day, all those philosophical questions become irrelevant. Never give up. Remember to survive! If you survive, there will be time to seek and find happiness, and if your time of happiness allows, maybe those other questions will help you find the meaningfulness behind your happiness."

"And if I get a good home?" Eros asked since the possibility of a good home for him seemed to be getting more and more remote as he got older.

"Maybe you can find the questions you are looking for, maybe not." For the first time, Skylark was equivocating with him. "Everyone and everything in natural reality has limits. You have come to my limits! There is no guarantee that you will find a dog or human with broader perspectives. You might find yourself having no one to talk to but chickens…or a human with a chicken brain!" (Skylark thought immediately of her first owner, and for the first time, she smiled as she thought of him with a chicken head.)

"Eh!" Eros gagged but subsequently smiled at the thought of talking with a chicken forever. In his discussions with the barn animals, chickens were the least beneficial conversationalists, to put it politely.

This chat with his mother left Eros with a feeling of uncertainty. Should he focus on the Way of the dog and survival and forget all this other stuff? Was it even worth pursuing this other stuff, even if he found a good home? Does the mantra answer all the questions that the Way of the dog does not?

Over the next two days, Eros learned the true definition of ambivalence—the depth of one's happiness equaled by the depth of one's sadness. With Charley's passing, his previous ideas about happiness now appeared superficial.

These ideas from his puppyhood, Eros suspected, were based mainly on stoicism, yet his stoicism felt like a precipice where happiness had to stop along the edge of emotions and the abyss of reality. Eros had to believe that there were more philosophies beyond stoicism, a place where one could find more happiness beyond this cliff. Eros only had more questions now, but for him, questions never ended. He needed more answers.

Eros was still a puppy. He had developed a lot of physical strength and gained a lot of insight. When he was young (yes, he thought he was *old* now), he used to think eating in paradise and playing in the kennel was the height of happiness, but that was when he was under the illusion that this paradise-like existence was the whole of reality, and there was nothing beyond the walls of the house.

Eros found more happiness in his relationships and a deeper appreciation of what they meant and how little time that life allowed for those relationships to flourish. When it came to Charley, Eros found it ironic that death led to learning to love better. If he wanted it, he could transform his life so that he loved more, and he wanted this, even in the face of change.

Finally, it happened. When Artemis was just under five months old, Mary burst through the house doors, swept up Artemis, a rug, and a crate, and retreated before one could pee on a tree. After both Artemis and Eros quickly said, "I love you," to each other, Artemis was taken, and Eros would never see her ever again.

The familiar conflict—his desire to have Artemis back and his happiness for Artemis's future—didn't last long. Grief tried to push happiness away, but Eros decided to commit to happiness, recognizing his desires to extend his sadness for their selfish origins of wanting change to stop. Eros began to view his sadness as an indulgence.

Happiness and sadness connect somehow in some aetherical realm, and to have one you have to have both. Sadness was necessary, and one had to embrace it when it was needed; however, to live forever in sadness is a choice. No one should choose sadness as a way of life, and Eros decided to follow his own advice.

*Of course, most dogs are resilient in this way. Humans are not, but humans are not as smart as dogs. Understanding and appreciating the simplicity of emotions and making clear decisions about them is a dogdom strength,* Eros thought a little arrogantly.

Later that day after Artemis's departure, Skylark came to talk with Eros.

"How are you, Eros?" Mother asked.

"It's the Way of the dog," Eros replied with a wry smile.

"I'm glad you're okay," Skylark said and smiled back.

"Mama, when will I be going?"

"Don't worry. Your time will come!" Mother assured him. "Your journey will start soon, but maybe it has already begun."

Eros did not appreciate this hint. All he knew was that his time did not come right away.

During this period of his life, once he vanquished sadness, loneliness (the sister of sadness) reared her ugly head. Compared to death, loneliness was a smaller challenge but a little more insidious.

Eros came to the realization that his desire for companionship and the lack of fulfillment when it came to these desires were transient. This emotion was simply a distraction that Eros felt he could do without as he waited for his journey to begin. Eros's tussle with this emotion did not last because his dog-based philosophy worked well.

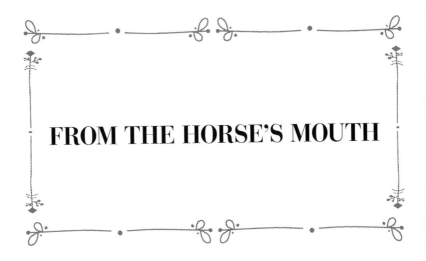

# FROM THE HORSE'S MOUTH

F ive days after Artemis had departed on her journey, Mary decided she could let Eros out again as long as Skylark was out with him, scouring the sky. Once out, Eros looked at Skylark, and glanced at Hercules on the other side of the yard. Then, he looked back at Skylark. Without mingling, his mother just nodded her head, and he was on his way.

This simple nod spoke volumes about their relationship. His mother recognized that Eros was moving into the pseudo-adult world of the juvenile. She had to believe that she had performed her duties as well as she could in bringing up Eros, and she had to trust him to do the right thing.

This didn't mean that his mother stopped caring. She cared deeply for all twenty-two pups that she had born over the years.

Every single one! She still cared for the three pups that had passed away, including Charley.

As she would have for any of her pups, she diligently watched the sky as Eros went across the yard to the paddock. She was pleased to notice Eros looking up regularly, checking for the hawk, and she was relieved that there was no shadow hanging over their yard anymore.

Eros jauntily dashed to the corral and barked at Hercules with a friendly bark.

"Hi, Eros," Hercules snorted. "Happy to see you about!"

"Hi, Hercules," Eros replied. Time and philosophy had returned Eros to a state of equanimity. Equanimity can arise from many conditions, but in this case, he was balancing the tension between his emotions about his current reality and his expectations for his future. However, this equanimity did not exclude pride.

Hercules bowed his head. Charley's departure had affected him too. Silently, the two animals communed on his passing. Then they moved on.

"What do you think about God?" Eros queried, abruptly, breaking the moment.

"I'm glad you have found some peace." Hercules nodded.

"Because I know the Way of the dog, I know everything!" Eros haughtily declared, strutting up to the horse paddock. "And I am calm—"

"You know nothing, Eros." Hercules laughed at this pompous little puppy. Nodding vigorously, he decided to open up about himself. "Mary is not my first owner. I was once owned by a nice old lady, and when she died, I was sold to Mary. My first owner was Eva."

"I don't know much about your history," Eros acknowledged. "But I really want to know your thoughts about God!"

"This old lady was tall and lithe and liked to ride me when I was young," Hercules said, reminiscing. "My, I was a wonderful stallion!"

"Do you believe in God? Mira doesn't!" Eros insisted, wondering why it took him this long to ask Hercules this question, which had become a standard in his repertoire of questions for everyone else. Since Hercules had been the first he had questioned, Eros assumed he hadn't perfected his survey questions on this subject, which was an adequate explanation for the exclusion.

"Eva was a handsome woman for her age." Hercules ignored Eros. "Small breasted, she had a penchant for tops with horizontal stripes. I believe in her youth she was athletic. Being vain, she wore wigs because her hair had become straggly, and she was embarrassed by it. And she had glasses that made her look wise, and on occasion she was. Most times she thought she was not."

"And I'm a little impatient pup," Eros said, jostling Hercules back to the present, wondering where the horse was heading with all this.

"She dabbled in philosophy books." Hercules started to have fun, teasing Eros by ignoring him. "She knew many philosophies, but she embraced a philosophy of live and let live. She considered this laissez-faire perspective the thought behind the American philosophy of 'life, liberty, and the pursuit of happiness.'"

"Hercules!" Eros was beyond exasperated, stamping all four of his paws sequentially in frustration, which was a hilarious sight.

"This is who I learned from, and I learned about stoicism, which you clutch around you like a shield." Hercules casually sauntered to his conclusion. "To be exact, you are sometimes stoic, and sometimes you are something else—really a bunch of something elses."

Mirabelle had said the same thing, Eros recalled.

"If the Way of the dog is stoicism, then yes, that's what the world is about!" Eros declared confidently, but he should have realized by now that his confidence was based on the foundation of an imperfect philosophy.

"There is no such thing as the perfect stoic. I call your mother's brand of philosophy soft stoicism."

"Soft?"

"A hardcore stoic would never cry," Hercules replied.

"But my mother did when Charley..." Eros trailed off, not able to say out loud that Charley was dead.

"Correct, but not being exactly stoic doesn't mean you aren't mostly stoic."

"But without the way, there is nothing else!" Eros showed a wee bit of desperation. He whined, almost whimpering. "You're *not* answering my question. What about God?"

"Far from that, young pup!" Hercules decided to put Eros out of his misery and answer his question. "You are rich with philosophical options and don't know it. There are thousands of philosophies! Not all but many of them talk about what God is."

"Thousands?"

"Maybe more! Some say philosophies are like snowflakes with each creature having their own, and like snowflakes philosophies can melt and refreeze as they pass through life. Your snowflake changes! One day you may find that stoicism isn't enough. Your snowflake has melted in the heat of life, and your philosophy is no longer the same, whether you want it to be or not."

"Mother says our Way is *the* Way," Eros said, retreating to his philosophical comfort zone. "I will always follow what my mother says!"

"Do you always do what your mother says?"

"No," was Eros's surly reply, thinking of his many surreptitious travels around the farm, all of which would have been against his mother's wishes.

"Why are you determined to do what your mother tells you in this case?" Hercules said and chuckled. "Unlike what you did with your mother, you can't sneak around and keep secrets from yourself!"

Eros turned sullen and silent.

"*Your* Way is the Way?" Hercules forged on. "You do it because your mother's philosophy is all you know now, and at this point, it is all you want to know. But reality may have different plans for you that require a different philosophy, especially when you find inconsistencies in Skylark's."

Eros recalled some suspicions that had arisen from Skylark's teaching. Owls are decapitators? Deer eating dogs? Deer eating *men*? These were part of his mother's teachings, but he was uncomfortable about their verity.

"You are going to find that some of the stuff your mother taught you is...inaccurate." Hercules stated this fact as gently as he could. It was as if he were reading Eros's mind, and he might have been. Regardless, Hercules proceeded cautiously. "Not every philosophy is completely right or completely wrong."

"But I have been taught that the Way of the dog is perfect, and that dogs are the chosen creatures on this earth."

"You have been taught the Way of the dog, but your mother's version is unique, a snowflake version of stoicism for her, which will never be exactly what you believe or what the original stoics intended. Your own experiences will mold your own philosophy regardless of the school of thought or religion you end up with."

"When humans refer to other humans as snowflakes, isn't that being mean?"

"Yes, another instance of humans abusing words that don't deserve it. Snowflakes are beautiful!" Hercules answered Eros's stack of questions. "And, *no*, every creature is a chosen creature. Otherwise it wouldn't be alive."

"Mama does have some odd things to say about some animals in the Wild," Eros admitted, sitting down and scratching his ear with his hind leg.

"Your mother is a wonderful creature, but if you find something erroneous in your mother's teaching, don't throw out her whole philosophy. Keep the good."

"But my mother is perfect!" Eros adamantly maintained.

Hercules could not help but laugh and whinny at Eros. Hercules had a very good time, prancing about in his corral and chuckling over the little dog's last comment.

"You'll learn, little pup," Hercules continued after controlling his snorts and involuntary neighs. "There are only two certainties in reality—death and the fact that there is nothing perfect in natural reality."

Eros was a little miffed. He thought that Hercules was laughing at him.

"You're not perfect, I'm not perfect, and your mother is not perfect!" Hercules tried to assuage Eros's feelings. "Not being perfect doesn't make us less than what we are!"

"I'll have to think about that." Struggling with Hercules's double negative, Eros retreated to his thoughts, clinging to the idea that his mother was perfect.

"In regard to *God*," Hercules said, emphasizing each phrase before he continued, "you dig deep as usual, Eros. A lot of what Mira says is…interesting. I don't know what to think, but I do know what I think God is not. Let me recite a little limerick."

## A Lazy Limerick about God

I know God is not here
and God is not there.
Some say God is everywhere,
but if everywhere is here or there,
then God is not anywhere.

Hercules pronounced the title with exquisite care before rattling through the limerick itself.

"Why do they call it lazy?"

"I think it has something to do with the poem not rhyming strictly according to the limerick rules," Hercules speculated.

"Whose rules? Human, dog, or God?"

"Got me. Rules are made to be broken. That's my motto! Does it really matter who makes them?" Hercules chomped on some hay before continuing. "Whether you are a believer in God or not, every philosopher tries to explain this enigmatic ditty."

"Is this a distraction, or are you going to tell me if you believe in God or not?" The relentless pup would not let go of his little intellectual bone.

"I'm going with the stoics on this one, but this means I wax philosophical," Hercules warned. "Can you handle that?"

"I think I can," Eros said but hesitated, clearly showing through his body language that he was not.

"Okay, but if I see your eyes roll back into their sockets or if you just get bored, I'll stop!" Hercules snickered. "I'm going to snort really loud after I'm done in case you want to skip over my conversation."

"Err, oh…" Hercules ignored Eros's stammering.

"Here goes, and here is how my end snort will sound." Bobbing his head up high, it came down with a huge *snort*! (This was one impressive sound, which even Skylark heard on the other side of the barnyard.)

"The stoics from the eastern Mediterranean and the later Roman philosophers that followed stoicism searched for the stuff of all stuff and believed this stuff to be living. When this living stuff manifested, they theorized that the manifestation could be many and varied. You could call it Everythingness." Hercules took a sip of water from a nearby trough. "You still with me?"

Eros looked dazed.

"Some technically call this materialistic pantheism, but I call this term malarkey. There's nothing materialistic about the living stuff," Hercules continued. Now that he was started, he was going to finish regardless of Eros's ability to understand. "Some would call their manifestation of this living stuff God, others Nothingness. Some may see just natural reality, while others see a rich tapestry of culture and religion."

Eros seemed about to teeter over. He appeared to be leaning on nothing.

"I believe in the living stuff of Everythingness and Nothingness," Hercules summarized. "Which means that I believe that God can manifest or not, depending on the philosophy that I am exploring at the time. Does that answer your question?"

Eros was catatonic.

"*Snort!*"

Eros was startled by the snort and fell over. He regained his feet quickly.

"Glad you're back with me," Hercules joked. "I'm not like the pigs. It was lonely talking to myself."

"And…" Eros stammered while he was recovering from his bout of severe boredom. "What about you? What is your philosophy?"

"I know so many philosophies that I have none," Hercules admitted. "Each has good parts and not-so-good pieces. Like dogs, horses, and people, no philosophy is perfect, but I have found that none really answer that limerick sufficiently either. So I keep looking."

"So you want me to be like you?"

"No, Eros, I want you to be like you. You are too metaphysically inclined to be contained by one philosophy—unless your life turns to constantly surviving day after day." Hercules clarified this point by adding, "Survival simplifies all philosophies!"

"My mother has basically said the same thing," Eros agreed. Hercules nodded his head, acknowledging Eros's interjection.

Hercules focused on Eros's green eyes. "Yet even through adversity, I can still envision you asking endless questions, and if life allows, your philosophy will expand inevitably."

"Are you saying I'll probably grow beyond the stoical philosophy that my mother has taught to me?"

"Yes, yes!" Hercules nodded his huge head.

"Why me? I'm just a little puppy!"

Hercules reluctantly continued, "Eros, don't blab this around, but I think you are smarter than me. And I know you are smarter than you think you are!"

This was quite an admission for a horse that placed the horse at the center of his universe and recognized horses as the wisest animals on the earth.

"You know a lot more than me," Eros modestly replied.

"That's experience, not wisdom," Hercules countered.

"I'm just a little dog."

"Every creature forgets that there is not just this philosophy or that philosophy. Whether based on traditional or religious philosophies, men and beasts are philosophical snowflakes, even though they may cluster together, afraid of being perceived separately."

"Like philosophical snowballs?" Eros piped up, smiling at the analogy.

"Yes," Hercules whinnied, amused, but he forged on to finish his thought. "In the end, each being has only his or her unique philosophy. Even if you hide in a snowball, you have your own unique snowflake. Eros, you are not afraid to be seen apart from others."

"And how can I be wise enough to better understand all these philosophies?" Eros was still not convinced. "Shouldn't I stay what I am?"

"No matter how desperately anyone tries, no one stays the same," Hercules stated. "When you transcend what you are today, you will be who you are tomorrow. I believe you will be a wiser version of you, and you won't be little anymore."

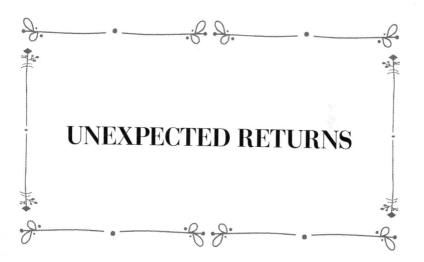

# UNEXPECTED RETURNS

As would come to pass, Eros was out in the yard on a warm late autumn day. The cars were buzzing past on the other side of the big field, and the cocks were crowing on the other side of the barn. Though starting very late because of the warm autumn, geese were flying above in a V-shaped formation, returning to their winter quarters. And there were no hawks!

Since there was no one to play with, Eros just basked in the sunshine, lying on a dry patch of ground. Then he heard distant brakes screeching and a horn honking from beyond the pasture. Curious as any dog would be, he looked in that direction, not needing to move a muscle. From his prone position, Eros could see a small fuzzy dot hop on and over the stone wall. Although he had excellent vision, the form of this object eluded his recognition.

This unknown entity, just a blob smudging the gray stone wall, was difficult to see because the fuzzy object was yellow and brown, camouflaged by the leaves scattered about from the fallen autumn foliage. But the object moved, and this movement was what captivated Eros's attention.

When Eros realized that the entity was coming toward the house, he moved from his prone position to an upright stance to better study this undefined creature. Eros's higher point of view allowed him to identify the object as some sort of big, fuzzy mammal—bristling with fur, and moving briskly toward the house.

Eros let out with a couple of warning yips to give his mother a heads-up and to warn this dubious beastie that he was a ferocious little dog, ready to defend Charley's territory to the death, but he was amenable to a peaceful solution, such as the strange creature departing quietly. (Do you see how precise a couple of yips can be?)

Since Eros was expecting to leave at any moment (at least in his mind he was), he could not accept that he had inherited the farm from Charley upon his friend's death. For him, this was still Charley's territory. He could not pretend otherwise.

Whatever this beast was, the creature did not respond to Eros's warnings and continued to approach the house.

"Bow-wow-wow," Eros alerted the farm of this possibly dangerous anomaly. His yips had decidedly deepening to wows as he grew older, but on occasions such as this, they still squeaked a bit. With this round of communications, the friendlier options of the previous yips were taken off the table, but the creature did not display any hostility, other than its relentlessness.

Skylark came out of the house because she had heard Eros. (Mary had not.) Mother asked Mary to open the door, but Skylark's nervousness piqued Mary's curiosity, so she went into the yard too.

"What's going on, Eros?" Skylark asked.

"Something pretty big is approaching the farm," he replied to his mother, pointing at the far end of the field with his nose. "I can't quite make out what it is."

"I see it," Skylark acknowledged. "I'm getting older, so my eyes aren't as good as yours. You will need to give me updates."

"I'm guessing it's a weasel." Eros crunched his eyes to try to see better. "But a weasel has darker brown fur, doesn't it?"

"Yes, I can see the color, and it isn't a weasel," Skylark confirmed.

"How about a bobcat?" Eros queried.

"Yes, they could have that coloring," Skylark hypothesized. "But the gait is not right."

Skylark and Eros stood at the house door, intent on this oncoming beast. Mary and Hercules followed the dog's eyes, and they were both drawn into watching.

"Looks like a little wooly mammoth," Hercules mocked from his paddock.

When the object got to the big stone in the middle of the field, the creature stopped. To their astonishment, the critter lifted his hind leg to pee on the Big Turd.

"It's…it's a big, hairy poodle! A monster poodle!" Eros shouted.

Lo and behold, a huge miniature poodle emerged from this mist of his mind. The distance made the dog look much larger by the growth of uncut hair. Although about twenty pounds, which was pretty large for a miniature poodle, this dog looked like he was forty pounds because of his wild hair growth. Eros was not sure if he should attack or welcome the beast!

Skylark was aghast! She could recognize the pee stance of all her pups, and she recognized this one.

"Charley," Skylark exploded. "You're *alive*?"

Mary, Eros, and Hercules were stunned, and then all hell broke loose. Skylark and Eros began barking joyously, while Hercules snorted and neighed nonstop. Mary just cried as Charley launched himself into her waiting arms.

This joyousness was a wave, engulfing the farmyard, and it passed to the rest of the animals on the farm. The joyousness spread like a warm summer breeze. Soon every animal on the farm was squealing and bleating and crowing and snorting and joining in the celebration, and many had no idea why.

All these animals may not have known the cause of the merriment, but when this joy was shared with them, they welcomed the feeling and desired to share the joy they felt in turn with others. Joy is an infection every creature desires!

Just as everything recedes, joy went out like a tide, but all the creatures had risen with this tsunami. This large wave of joy passed over the farm, leaving the residue of joy—happiness—glowing over every creature, even the mice, ants, and chickens.

---

Mary's crying continued, but Skylark's and Eros's barking had ceased. They wished to excitedly chat with Charley, but the emotions of the moment interfered with their mingling, as Charley's emotions prevented him from communicating as he came up to the house. Soon the farm was quiescent, and Mary stopped crying.

"My, my, Charley, you need some grooming!" Mary choked out her first words. "Let me go get the clippers."

"Charley, how?" Skylark asked the obvious question after Mary put the wayward pup down and trotted off, looking for the grooming clippers. "We all thought you were dead."

"It's a long story," Charley said and scratched his sides. Eros believed he saw some black dots in Charley's fur and stepped away a bit. There was a good chance that Charley had fleas. He thought to himself, *Mary will fix that!*

"Mary is going to be right back, so I'll give you the short version. I survived the fall because of some tree branches and bushes. It wasn't pretty. I came out really bruised and sore, but nothing was broken. A damn miracle!" Charley accentuated *damn* with a growling bark! "Then the damn bird came down." Again, he gave that growling bark. "And I had to fight it off. This was quite a battle, and eventually, the bird gave up to look for easier prey."

Skylark was quiet about Charley's use of bad words, which Eros was okay with. He preferred Charley swearing and alive rather than absent and dead.

"I survived the hawk on instinct and strength," Charley continued. "But during the fall, I bumped my head a couple times, and after the battle with the hawk, I discovered I had amnesia. For a few days, I had no idea who I was or where I was going."

"Ah, that explains why we had this feeling of uncertainty about your death," Skylark exclaimed. As their telepathy was sensitive to emotions, it was also bound to identity. Amnesia and the sense of identity clouded could easily mimic the telepathic message that Charley had died.

"After the amnesia wore off, I spent the rest of the time smelling the area and looking to get back to the farm," Charley explained, smiling. "I followed the smell of the pigsty. Once I locked onto that, I knew where home was."

"You must have had lots of adventures," Eros said with some envy.

"Most of which I wish I hadn't had." Charley seemed wiser than the dog he was before he had left. "For one thing, for most of the adventure, I had no food. Even now I'm starving!"

Mary returned with her clippers, but before the house door closed, Charley evaded her and ran into the house to sit in paradise near the dog bowls. Mary followed him in, and so did his entourage, Skylark and Eros.

"Ah," Mary nodded. "I suppose you need to be fed first and then clipped."

With that, she put down her grooming tools and put out food for Charley. He must have been famished because he ate two bowls' worth, and in this little task, Charley found happiness.

# TIME HAS COME FOR...

**E**ros celebrated his six-month birthday, but he was ambivalent about it. With Charley's return, he felt more than ever that Charley should be there at the farm and that Eros should not be, yet he was here and could not deny that fact.

Eros was in the midst of waiting for his journey to begin, but he was not sure what he was waiting for. To be whisked away to a new owner? To not be whisked away? To find elusive happiness? Or to live by scraping just enough together to survive? Or maybe he was happy now and didn't know it. (Of dogs and men, this was a common trap that he didn't want to fall into.) This waiting and the accompanying worrying had been carrying on for some time.

During this time, Eros spent a considerable amount of time with Hercules, but these philosophical discussions did not relieve his confusion in this matter. During this time, Eros concluded, *Philosophy does not have all the answers.* Eventually, he would have to accept that he missed his departed siblings. He thought, *You can only do this for yourself; no one and no philosophy can do this for you.*

Charley resumed his sentinel duties, now integrating a sky watch in his routine. Mary was busy with her household chores, and Eros suspected that Skylark was pregnant. Eros assumed her pregnancy happened shortly after Matt's departure. Eros recalled that Skylark had left the farm for a week. Instinctively, he understood her absence was related to a new pregnancy as he sensed a change in her odor upon her return.

The overall message of these changes about Eros was that he envisioned himself as being pushed to the periphery of life on the farm, where even talking with the chickens appeared inviting. *Alienation finds odd friends,* he reasoned.

Eros felt that something should be happening. He could sense the change in his mother. He could sense the change in Charley, his presence emanating a more complete competence, changing the social chemistry in the barnyard. Change was everywhere, but nothing appeared to be changing in his situation.

Soon, Eros knew, he would be an afterthought in his Mother's and Charley's lives, an anachronism. Skylark would go on to a new brood of pups that needed her complete attention, and Charley would go on to perfecting his idea of being an alpha dog. Eros would be the odd doggie, the eccentric uncle that nobody wanted around, writing books that no one read.

Feeling he was a leftover misfit, Eros kept up the ritual of telling Skylark, Charley, and Mary that he loved them first thing in the morning and the last thing at night. These targets of his love had gotten very involved in the next phase of their lives, but he adhered to his principles. They were so busy that Eros doubted that they heard him, but he persevered.

In this instance, Eros refused to change. He would be damned (hope Skylark didn't hear that) if he loved less because they spent less time with him. On this one point, he was going to be a stubborn puppy. Eros was going to love them whether they wanted it or not!

Shortly after his six-month birthday, Eros asked his mother a question. "When will my journey begin?" On that first day, Eros asked four times. Mother brushed him off over and over. A day later, he started asking ten times, and by the third day, he was asking every fifteen minutes until his mother, maddened, finally responded.

"What if this is your journey?"

"Egad!" Eros was blossoming in his adolescence, and the thought of him staying at home with his parent was not on his list of ideal expectations. He didn't know what his expectations were, but he knew this was not one of them. Skylark did accomplish her goal with her pert response, as Eros stopped asking her that question for fear of getting the same answer.

That night Eros had an epiphany! He started to feel that he was not wanted. Someone wanted his brothers and sisters. Charley was wanted by Mary, but no one wanted Eros. Eros sat around the kennel and contemplated this irony. The fear of leaving had given way to the fear of not leaving. This reversal gnawed at him, bringing his emotions into a battle with his self-esteem.

Eros followed what he had done previously, putting the burden of his desires aside, but every time he wondered about his journey, this distraction would return forcefully. He kept putting it aside, and the fears kept coming back. Then he started to fear he was beginning to think like a human. *Am I going to allow myself to be sad forever?*

"Mama, Mama!" He ran to Skylark, alarmed, stating to her his conclusion. "I'm human!"

Once he explained to his mother what he meant, she laughed and laughed. Her laughter made him feel better. She laughed so much that it looked like she was choking to Mary, who had heard Skylark and had peeked into the kennel.

"Are you all right, Shyla?" Mary asked, wondering about this strange behavior.

"No, Eros," Skylark said after she composed herself, answering Mary by settling down with her big puppy. "You will never be as stupid as the stupidest human."

While his mother was still quietly giggling, Eros decided to broach a new topic. Since Artemis's departure, he had been accumulating questions, some of which he was hoping his mother would answer, but this was the first time he had had an opportunity to ask.

"Can I ask you a few questions?"

"Sure, but you rarely have just a few questions," Skylark casually responded.

"Have any of your other pups asked the questions that I ask?"

"No, my metaphysical one!" Mother continued her chuckling. "You have been the only one."

"I know we go to the Big Nap, but where do we go when we die?"

"You've asked that before, and I still don't know."

"How high is the sky?"

"I don't know."

After a pause, Eros said, "I'm confused."

"Everyone is confused, and if they say otherwise, they are lying to either you or themselves...or both."

Remembering that, according to Hercules, Skylark's knowledge was limited, Eros realized that the "I don't know" and "I believe" answers bounced off the outer frontier of her knowledge. For the first time, he acknowledged that his parent was not omniscient. If she was not omniscient, there was a chance that her teachings were imperfect.

Perfection is a fragile and fleeting instance, never lasting longer than a moment, if even then. No parent is perfect, although early on, every child assumes they are; however, for his puppyhood she was the most perfect mother he had ever known, and that was all that counted.

"Eros, I once told you that you could ask me a hundred questions," Mother said, almost smug. "And I told you that I would give you a hundred answers, but I never guaranteed that you would like the answers."

Eros concurred since he was not happy with the "I don't know" responses and still didn't know what to make of the "I believe" answers.

"Shyla," Mary called his mother over, interrupting their chat.

"Let me tell you about the stupidest humans." Skylark rushed to push out one last thought for her puppy. "The stupidest humans think they are the smartest. Don't aspire to be the smartest. It will make you stupid, and—worse—you will look like an imbecile in the process."

Answering Mary's call, Skylark was gone, but she had left Eros with a lot to think about. His concerns over the start of his own journey kept coming up. Doubt is a constant companion of the young, and Eros concluded that he must be stupid since he was trying to be so smart about his journey. Life's journey just happens regardless of anyone's concerns.

About a week later, Eros felt an unexpected excitement about the house when he woke up. After he had done his daily poop at the far corner of the kennel, he came rambling back toward the house, curious.

Suddenly, the door of the house burst open, and out popped Skylark, quickly followed by Mary. Skylark was prancing about, filled with eagerness. Mary moved with the alacrity and determination, which Eros had only seen three times before. Even Charley started hopping around.

Mary grabbed the bedding Eros had been using, a blue mat with a colorful insect pattern of huge ladybugs and dragonflies. With little loss of motion, she turned and nabbed the puppy. Before he knew it, Eros was in the crate with the door closed and latched. With a great deal of apprehension and excitement, Eros looked forward to his journey.

"I love you, Charley," Eros flung out the last thought that his brother and mother would hear from him. "I love you, Mama!"

"Love ya!" Charley replied. After his trials in the Wild, he had no trouble expressing his emotions. Charley told Eros after he returned, "Emotions are macho!"

"Keep on lovin', and I love *you*, Eros!" his mother replied, crying joyful tears, confirming forever her soft stoicism. "Remember—to live is to survive, and if you survive, you always have the chance to find happiness! Relentlessly seek joy and you will be rewarded!"

Eros's journey had begun, but this story is for another doggie day.

# EPILOGUE

Such is the way of life and metaphysics! Not all questions are answered, and the threat of the Wild remains unresolvable. Change takes people and pups whichever way it wishes. As in any struggle to know one's place in the universe, this story may seem small, but for this little dog it means everything.

From *The Book of the Dog*

> With fortitude, you can eventually find joy,
> Yet joy is transient, a phenomenon that passes!
> From joy's brief bloom, happiness will blossom;

As joy's residue, happiness can be endless.
When happiness overtakes you, as it will,
Understand that this is like a virulent infection,
Which you can pass indiscriminately to all.
In the first few days, as your euphoria expands,
Express your madness! Enthrall all you can!
Share as much of your happiness as possible.
If someone becomes ill with your infection,
This contagion can continue, inextinguishable.
And you can be reinfected by this affliction.

This is a poor human translation (as are most of the excerpts from *The Book of the Dog*) of the most beautifully written poem ever composed. As only a dog can do, every line has perfect meter, and the rhyming passes like a quiet stream, the waters dancing by in silent synchronization. Please forgive the efforts of this translator, for much has been lost in the translation.

Catching up to the science of dogdom, modern psychological research has discovered that happiness can be transmitted like a disease. Your happiness can infect the happiness of everyone around you. In turn, starting with your loved ones, your family's happiness can impact the world. This is the true power behind the butterfly effect.

Although not a humorist, I have attempted to infect you with the joy from my life. Hopefully, if this book has touched you with any residual happiness, please make an attempt to infect as many people as you can.

Although they are soft stoics, dogs cannot help but think positively, always. "As it will" refers to the unshakeable dogdom belief that happiness will *overtake* you regardless of your circumstances. (In fact, in most cases, happiness is already all around you, and you are just refusing to embrace it. *Stop ignoring happiness!*) Be the hero of your own story, and have the unconquerable faith in your own happiness!

I do.

Printed in the United States
By Bookmasters